THE RISE OF A DOPE BOY CHICK 2

SHONTAIYE MOORE

Cole Hart
SIGNATURE NOVELS

The Rise Of A Dope Boy Chick 2

Mailing List

To stay up to date on new releases, plus get information on contests, sneak peeks, and more,

Go To The Website Below...

www.colehartsignature.com

TEXT TO JOIN

To stay up to date on new releases, plus get exclusive information on contests, sneak peeks, and more...

Text ColeHartSig to (855)231-5230

ACKNOWLEDGMENTS

I just want to give a special thank you to the boss of Cole Hart Signature. You push me to do my best and motivate me to believe in myself. I'm truly grateful for the opportunity to work under your wing.. I also want to thank any reader that has taken the time to read a book by me. You may not know me yet, but I promise you will get to. My goal is to leave a mark in this publishing industry. Follow me on Facebook, Instagram, and Twitter.

Facebook: https://www.facebook.com/shontaiyeauthor

Instagram: https://www.instagram.com/shontaiyemoore/

Twitter: https://twitter.com/ShontaiyeMoore

Facebook Reading Group: Shontaiye Moore's Book Bar https://www.facebook.com/groups/1954612884663552/

❧ I ❧

Josiah's eyes fluttered at the sound of Asia's syrupy voice. With a vacant stare on his face, he finally looked up. He had been quietly lost in thought.

"Josiah, did you hear me? *I said*, Mitch is getting out tomorrow."

Hearing her repeat herself, forced him to snap out of it. The simple words that rolled from her lips were sure to change everything.

"Yeah, I heard you." He turned to face her. "Mitch is getting out tomorrow, and you need fifty-grand," he repeated.

He had to repeat the first part out loud since he was still having a bit of difficulty processing it. He wasn't expecting that kind of news so early in the morning. It was hard to determine if it was good news or bad news. *This is good news ...right*, he thought to himself. He should have been excited, but he would be lying if he said that he was.

Still in her blue, silk nightie, Asia walked towards the bed slowly and stood by its edge. As she leaned her curvy body against the tall, wooden bedpost, she couldn't help but notice Josiah's solemn expression. Although he had much love for his friend; Josiah still bore the look of disappointment on his face. A face that should have shown happiness and relief; instead, showed the opposite. It wasn't that he wasn't happy for Mitch, because deep down he was. He wouldn't wish jail amongst his worst enemy. Josiah was more confused and unsure about where that left him and Asia. *His* feelings for Asia were made very clear; however, he couldn't help but now question hers. Her initial reaction to the news is what caused him to worry. He glanced at her. Her beautiful light-brown face looked stunned, weary, and confused.

"I know it's a lot to digest," Asia said softly, feeling Josiah's eyes fixed on her.

She shuffled around nervously, adjusting her body weight from one foot to the other.

"Actually, it isn't a lot to digest," Josiah countered impatiently. "Not for me anyway. You know how I feel, and you know how I felt about telling Mitch long before this."

He wasted no time expressing his distaste for the situation. He wasn't particularly fond of her reaction either. Her expression revealed her doubts; leaving him no choice but to lay everything out on the table so they could be on the same page. Josiah had pushed himself all the way up in the bed and his back was now pressed against the king-size headboard. He wanted to look at her as she responded. The eyes always revealed lies and uncertainties. Asia quickly diverted her eyes away from Josiah's piercing gaze. She knew what he was looking for. She knew that he was studying her. As she looked off, she didn't respond right away. Instead, she uncomfortably pushed back a few of the loose strands of hair that were swept into her face as if they were affecting her ability to think properly.

"I don't know Josiah. I care about you but---"

"You *care* about me?" Josiah interjected, his face displaying a puzzled frown. He certainly wasn't expecting to hear that. Not those words.

"Before, you loved me ... Now, you just care about me," he said, growing agitated.

He wasn't one to throw shit up in a person's face after he did something for them; however, he almost did when Asia opened her mouth. He'd just bought her ass a car *and* a house! Now, because Mitch was coming home, she was suddenly confused. Josiah glared at Asia. The look on her face had the nerve to seemingly question his anger.

"Why is this even a discussion Asia? What changed?" He paused and continued to stare at her; his dark eyes burning a hole through her. Asia stood there uncomfortably while Josiah waited for a response. When one never came, he continued.

"You're grown Asia. Say how you feel," he encouraged. "I understand if you still love Mitch; that's only right; but, how you feel about me shouldn't be confusing to you. Circumstances shouldn't change how you feel about someone. If it does, then that leaves me reason to question your character. What does that make you?" he asked. It pissed him off that she was making Mitch's impending arrival a factor in where they stood in their relationship.

"I'm not saying that babe. It's just a lot to take in," she said.

She took a seat on the edge of the bed. With her body hunched forward, she quietly rubbed at her temples and then squeezed her eyes shut in frustration. This was the reason she had been hesitant to get involved with Josiah from the very beginning. As Mitch's friend, she knew that was a boundary that she shouldn't cross; however, with Josiah's heavy persistence and persuasion, she did it anyway. They were now in a fucking love triangle. She knew she was just as much to blame. Asia had no doubt that Mitch was going to consider them a couple as soon as he stepped out of that jail. How was she going to break the news to him that she was now sleeping with his friend?

"Look ... Mitch is going to call again to make sure things have been handled. Why don't you just tell him then? Or better yet, have him call me and I'll tell him. We can't let him come home and feel blindsided Asia," Josiah said.

He wanted to be clear that he still wanted to be with her,

regardless if Mitch was home or not. That was something the three of them all had to deal with like adults.

"Josiah ... Even if we tell him today, he's still going to feel blindsided. Once he asks how long shit has been going on, he's going to feel that way since it's been going on for months right under his nose."

"So ... You don't want to tell him?" Josiah asked, still partially confused as to where her argument was headed.

Her reluctance to inform Mitch about their relationship, was an instant blow to his ego. He was good enough to be with during Mitch's absence; he was good enough for her to accept his gifts; but he wasn't good enough for her to build a life with, in front of a man that had involuntarily left her with nothing. To him, she was basically choosing Mitch.

Asia sighed. "I'm not saying that ... I would just rather wait."

Josiah stared blankly for a minute and then shook his head with disdain. With his teeth clenched tightly, he abruptly scooted towards the edge of the bed and got up.

"Where you goin'?" Asia asked. Josiah had walked over to the dresser and began quickly gathering his things to get dressed.

"I'm about to slide out," he responded quietly.

Josiah's heart hammered in his chest, while anger roared through him like a tide. He did his best to control the feelings that were flooding him. He looked at Asia, and although angry; he couldn't help but gaze at her weakly. She was the other piece to his heart, and here she was ... telling him that she was unsure of whether she wanted to continue to be with him. Her feelings of confusion had him with feelings of turmoil. He thought Asia was his other half; yet, he was now learning that she was actually a weakness. Not only was she a weakness for him; she was also a weakness for Mitch.

Throughout his lifetime, he had seen close friends become enemies; all over a woman. He knew how Mitch felt about her. When he had convinced Asia to give him a chance, he did so with the assumption that Mitch would be locked up for many years to come. That he would eventually come to peace with their relationship. Now that he was getting out, Josiah realized how poor a choice he had made.

"Please don't be mad at me Josiah," Asia said softly, rising from her position on the bed and walking over to him where he was seated on the royal blue, chaise lounge that sat next to her closet. When she got in front of him, she stood quietly for a second and then reached out to stroke his face. To her surprise, he snatched his head away from her touch.

"I'm not mad," he said, clearly lying. Against his better judgement, he was going to let her do things her way. *For now, anyway*.

"I'm going to go get this money. I'll wire it to you."

He pulled on his second boot and stood up from the lounge.

"*Wire it?*" Her forehead crinkled in disbelief. She couldn't believe his childish behavior. "You're not coming back?"

Josiah stood in front of Asia and looked at her like she was a naked whore in a church pew.

"Why would I come back, Asia? Mitch is coming home. So, you expect me to spend the night with you here, and then tuck my tail between my legs and go back to Wilmington when he touches down. Or better yet ... you want me to spend the night and then go with you, to get him?" he asked sarcastically. "Either way, you got me fucked up," he continued angrily.

She was really testing his patience. He took a few quick breaths and quickly walked away with Asia hot on his heels.

"Why are you making it seem like I did something wrong?" she asked. "You knew this shit was fucked up from the beginning," she spat. She walked briskly behind Josiah as he walked through the condo and headed into the kitchen to grab his keys.

"How was it fucked up?" He stopped and turned around to face her. "Mitch put me in your life. He had hella years on his head. I mean ... At some point he knew someone was going to step to you and start fucking you."

"But not his friend, Josiah!" she scoffed.

Asia couldn't understand why Josiah felt that what they were doing was okay. Asia took responsibility for her role; however, Josiah made it seem like it was okay for him to come in and scoop up his friend's girl. No matter how Josiah tried to dress it up, it was foul. *You don't just spring that type of shit on people*, she thought.

Josiah stopped abruptly at the door and turned around to face Asia. "I'm not perfect. The circumstances and situation weren't ideal, but at the end of the day, I know my intentions. I didn't walk into your life on no malicious shit. I had no intention of fuckin' with you just because you were Mitch's girl. I ain't no foul-ass nigga. I'm human, and I got caught up. Instead of telling myself, don't chase you because you my nigga's baby-ma; I told myself that he'd appreciate and respect a real nigga in your life. *In his son's life*. I've done nothing but take care of you, be good to you, and show you love. Am I wrong for that?" he asked, while staring down at Asia.

Asia swallowed hard and forced back her desire to break down into tears. As he continued to peer down into her eyes, she couldn't help but look away. She didn't know what to do. Not only was she confused; she was also torn. She loved Mitch; she always would, but she was in love with Josiah. She knew at some point; she was going to have to choose. A part of her felt like her choice should automatically be the father of her child; however, her heart screamed for Josiah; yet choosing him felt like a betrayal. She didn't know if she wanted to betray Mitch ... or her heart. After staring at Asia and waiting for a response, Josiah realized that one would never come. He knelt and kissed Asia on her forehead; something he never did.

"I'm out," he said softly.

He turned his back, opened the door and walked out. Asia didn't bother to stop him. Breathing heavily and with her lips trembling, she did nothing as the door closed in her face. This was one of the toughest situations she had ever been in. Fighting Muff at the mall, being flat broke with her son, getting kicked out of her own house, even finding out Waleek had been arrested for murder, didn't compare to what she felt. Her heart was heavy, and her stomach felt as if she had been kicked in it. She had no idea what to do. Was she going to be with Mitch when he came home, or was she going to admit to him that she was now with Josiah?

❦

FROM HIS SPOT at the round table, Mitch looked past his Spades opponent and glanced at the digital clock on the wall. He knew he had to have already checked it at least one hundred times. His lawyer had come and visited him earlier that morning around 9 a.m. and since then, he couldn't seem to sit still. After hearing the news that his appeal had been granted, he called Asia and then immediately began to pack up. It had literally taken him only twenty minutes to gather up all his valuables and secure them in a thin, white, plastic trash bag. Now, the time was dragging painfully slow.

Mitch did his best to occupy himself with various activities; he tried taking a long shower, reading a few magazines out of his collection, and even watching some television. However, that did nothing to speed his day along. He looked back over at the clock and it was only approaching noon. He'd just eaten lunch and had only been at the card table fifteen minutes, and he was already back to watching the clock. He wished the day would hurry the fuck up.

He couldn't help but feel jittery and nervous. He had been gone nearly two years and he knew a lot had changed. He was excited about any and everything. Most importantly, he was eager to see the home Asia had created. He'd seen pictures of the new condo she was leasing, but he couldn't wait to see it in person. He couldn't wait to take a real shower, *in a real bathroom*; sink his toes in the plush carpet that she had just installed in her bedroom. He couldn't wait to be back with his family; hold his son, kiss his mother, and eat a real meal. The simple luxuries most men took for granted, he couldn't wait to have again. He made a vow to himself that if he got out, he would never return. He meant it. He planned to drag out his appeal for as long as he could, and when he couldn't drag it out any longer, he planned to fight with everything he had.

He refused to leave Asia and Hasan again. He knew he would have his work cut out for him because successful appeals and second trials were costly. He'd spent a lot of money just to get this far. He knew in order to win this time; he'd need to make sure he continued to keep the money coming in. The daycare and a regular job weren't going to cut it. Only drug money would suffice for the massive amount of legal fees he would accumulate.

After getting beat several times in his game of Spades, he retired to his cell and lay flat on his bunk. There was nothing more for him to do now, besides sleep the remaining hours away. When he woke the next morning, and they called his name, he would be a free man. He couldn't wait.

2

Later that day, Josiah exhaled a deep, weary breath and pulled up against the curb of his bakery in Wilmington. While he was leaving Asia's, Trish had called him and informed him that they had an emergency that required him to come in right away. She wouldn't tell him much over the phone. That alone worried him. If it wasn't one thing, it was another. He didn't feel like hearing more bullshit. Going back and forth with Asia earlier already had his head hurting. He took a deep breath and tilted his head back towards the ceiling. The action was pointless, since it wasn't going to help his damn headache one bit.

After allowing his car to idle for a few minutes, he turned it off and snatched the key from the ignition. He quickly glanced around cautiously. Sensing no type of danger, he pulled back the door handle and stepped out of the vehicle. When Josiah walked into Sweet Treats, he immediately knew something was wrong. His eyes quickly darted around, but he didn't see anyone. The place was deathly quiet, and he didn't smell any of the familiar aromas that normally wafted through the air.

"Trish! Where you at?" he called out, as he slowly walked around the empty lobby.

He remembered seeing her car outside, so it was odd that she wasn't in the front where she was usually assisting their small staff. Trish was very hands-on and was also typically one of the first faces one would see when they walked through the door. After realizing no one was nearby, he pushed through the door and proceeded to the entrance that led to the front counter, kitchen, and offices.

"I'm back here," Trish yelled for the second time.

Josiah hadn't heard her at first. He followed her voice into the office. When he walked in, she was seated quietly at her desk. Her computer was off, along with the lights. The place looked gloomy and unusually dark. Her face was solemn, and her chin was resting lightly on the back of her tiny hand. He could tell something was weighing heavily on her mind. Despite her weary look, Trish still looked stunning. She always did. Even in her white bakery uniform. At one point, Josiah thought that she would be a viable candidate for a wife; however, after a year of dating, he realized she wasn't the one. She wasn't his speed and felt more like a sister than a lover. A petite, toasted-brown beauty with angelic features, she was certainly beautiful in her own right. A friend of his sister's since high school; she was college-educated, goal-oriented and focused. Unfortunately, she bored Josiah. She didn't have the spunk, charm and wit that he yearned for.

"What's up Trish? Where's everyone?" he asked softly as he stepped inside the room. It felt more like the temple of doom. "Why you got it so dark in here?" he asked, looking around with a frown.

He had a feeling that whatever she was about to say was going to be some heavy shit. Josiah plopped down in one of the office chairs that sat across from Trish's desk. The building itself was small, so the office of course, was even tinier. It held her tiny oak desk, a few chairs, some office equipment, and a storage cabinet containing all their important files and contracts.

"I sent everyone home, because there was an incident today.

Well, an incident that happened yesterday, but I'm just getting all the details today."

"An incident? What kind of incident?" Josiah asked.

"Ethan wrecked the van," she said with a weary sigh.

"What? How did he manage to do that?" Josiah asked in disbelief. He already knew who she was talking about since the business was small. They had two people who worked the front counter and only four drivers. He distinctly remembered Ethan, since he was their only white driver.

"He fell asleep on the road," she replied hesitantly.

Trish pushed back her thick, shoulder-length hair, looked at Josiah and waited nervously for his response. She felt like she was to blame, and she had let him down. She hated letting him down. Trish expected him to be angry. Ethan had been complaining for weeks about his struggle to juggle his heavy course-load, in addition to his work schedule. Her initial response was to offer him more money; however, Josiah advised her to find an additional driver. To him, her response to Ethan's simple request was silly. He didn't say he had *financial* problems; he said he needed more rest. The intelligent response would have been to cut his hours and ask the other drivers to pick up the extra load until she could find another driver. In their line of business, those type of mistakes couldn't afford to be made. They had the potential to bring down everything.

She never mentioned it to Josiah, but she too was tired. She had been running the bakery all by herself since it had been opened nearly two years back when he first got out of jail. Most of his business endeavors were her idea. Up until recently, she felt appreciated. Before, Josiah would be in and out, but she still could depend on him to help her run things at the bakery. Lately, she could barely reach him. He always claimed to be busy and tied up. Seemed to her that his only priority was making more money. But where did she fit in? When was anyone going to start thinking about Trish? Those were the two questions she found herself constantly asking. She'd been there for him but when was he going to start being there for her.

A part of her felt an immense sense of loyalty to him and his family. She'd met Josiah's sister Maria, her freshmen year of high school. They immediately clicked and since her mother worked two jobs as a single mom, Maria's family saw something in her and welcomed her with open arms. It didn't sit well with Josiah and Maria's mother that Trish would often go home to an empty house and go to bed without a home-cooked meal. Even though Trish had a good mother who did the best she could, she still would often go without. That stopped when she became a part of Maria's family. Josiah was rising up the ranks and he made sure everyone had everything they needed. It had been that way ever since. Even when their attempt at a relationship failed, it had still been that way. Up until recently. While she still had Josiah's financial support, she no longer had his mental support. He simply wasn't present.

"What did they find in the van?" Josiah asked, snapping Trish out of her brief thoughts. He was no longer sitting back comfortably in his chair; he was now sitting upright; his back stiff and rigid, while he waited for her response.

Trish looked around the office cautiously as if she had to tell him something but couldn't, because she didn't know who was listening. She then got up unexpectedly and closed the door to the small office. The police had already stopped by earlier, but she wouldn't allow them to step foot behind the counter. She had no doubt that they probably bugged the front. She had closed the door to ensure that what they said, had no chance of being accidentally picked up. After shutting the door, she walked over to where Josiah was seated, leaned down and whispered in his ear.

"Ten bricks," she said, with a hard swallow.

Josiah's body seemed to freeze in place and for a moment, he almost felt like he had stopped breathing.

"Fuck." More bullshit, just like he'd expected. "Where's

Ethan?" he asked.

"They're holding him at James T Vaughn, in Smyrna," she replied. "He has no bail. I'm assuming because of the amount of product."

"Damn ... But that's good for us because that won't allow him to come snooping for information. The first thing they would do in a case like this is to put a wire on him."

"*Good?*" Trish couldn't help but snap back her neck and frown up her face at Josiah in disbelief. "He's a fuckin' kid Josiah!" she said, angrily smacking the wooden desk with her fist.

"I know that," he replied sharply. He wasn't trying to hear what she had to say. Things were bad enough. That was one of the reasons they weren't together. She always wanted to argue. Despite her role in his drug operations, Trish did her best to operate with some sense of morale. If she didn't agree with something; she had no problem making it known.

"For God's sake Josiah; it would be different if he was a hustler off the street," she continued. "But this is a kid who was just trying to make some money and get his education. A kid with a bright future. A kid that didn't know he was running *your* fuckin' drugs!"

Josiah knew what she was trying to do; she was trying to make him feel bad, and it was working. He wasn't proud of the way he moved his drugs, but to him, it was the safest way. He had four drivers and none of them knew there were drugs in the van. They were all under the impression that they worked for a legitimate, law-abiding business. Drug runners were typically caught because they were nervous and fucked up. A person that didn't know they were running drugs was far less likely to be nervous and careless. The method had worked for years. Unfortunately, Josiah nor Trish ever considered the unfavorable effects of a sleepy driver.

"What do you want me to do Trish?" he asked, while quickly leaning forward and angrily throwing up his hands. "You want me to go to the fuckin' jail and tell them, *they're my drugs?* If so, you've lost your mind. What I *will* do ... is the same thing that *he's* probably doing. I'm going to deny knowing that they were there. They can't prove shit and Ethan doesn't know shit!"

"You don't know what Ethan knows," she mumbled.

"What the fuck is that supposed to mean?"

"It means exactly what I said. You don't know what Ethan knows! You don't know shit because you're never here! You're too busy running up and down the road to lay up with whores!" she yelled.

Trish went to continue, but Josiah jumped to his feet to leave. "Fuck this shit!" He wasn't about to argue with her. The shit was played out.

"Whatever Josiah," Trish said in disgust. "As usual, run from the problems you create while other people break their fuckin' neck to fix them."

Josiah went to respond, but Trish turned back around in her chair and put her back to him. She was done talking to him. To her, Josiah was getting sloppy. He wasn't tending to his business, and he was putting everyone at risk. She knew she was also at fault, but he still needed to be present. She couldn't do everything on her own. Lately, Maria had been telling her to move to Florida. Maria loved her brother, but she also wanted her friend Trish to be happy *and* safe. It was no secret that Josiah no longer wanted Trish on an intimate level. It seemed to everyone that he just kept her around because she was beneficial. Maria had been telling her to let go and move on. Not only did she not want to see her best-friend heartbroken; she also didn't want to see her locked away behind her greedy brother. Josiah had more than enough to retire comfortably, but he wanted to keep going. And he insisted on keeping Trish tucked away by his side to help him accomplish whatever he was trying to accomplish.

The police had already questioned Trish once. They even attempted questioning her a second time on the same day. That time, however, she had her lawyer pull up. It was simple; they wanted to know whose drugs were in the back of that van, and they weren't going to stop until they found answers — *or* someone gave them some.

"I suggest you lawyer up Josiah," Trish said softly, as she began rummaging through her desk and gathering up her things. "I already have. And ... I quit," she said, her face emotionless.

She was going to finally listen to her friend Maria. She wasn't going to jail behind Josiah's ass. He made it clear he didn't want to be with her; so, there was no need sitting in Wilmington being his rider. He could find another bitch to play that role.

"You what?" Josiah asked.

"You heard me. I'll have my things out in a few days. I'm going to Florida."

She didn't expect a response, and Josiah didn't even bother to give one. He wasn't begging her ass for anything. He walked out while she sat teary-eyed and continued to snatch open every drawer on her desk and pull out her belongings. She planned to take what she could carry and return for the rest of her things later.

❦

"WHAT THE HELL is going on Josiah!" Lolita asked her only son. He was her pride and joy, but sometimes he made her want to slap the shit out of him.

Her daughter Maria had just interrupted her while she stood in the kitchen, dancing to her Bluetooth speaker and preparing dinner. Needless to say; her attempt at living her best life had been interrupted. Maria walked into the kitchen and explained how she had just gotten a teary, heart-wrenching call from her best-friend Trish. Now Lolita needed to know what was going on. She'd be lying if she said, the two didn't have a reputation for being at odds; however, since they'd stopped dating and became business partners, they'd been doing well. Or so she thought.

"Mommy, please not now," Josiah groaned.

He had only been sitting idle in his car for twenty-minutes

and now she was calling with even more bullshit. His dark-brown eyes darted to the dashboard. The bright, neon-green letters shown 10:00 a.m. Josiah let out an exaggerated huff through his mouth and squirmed angrily against his leather seat. His day was going shitty. He had no doubt that his mother, who he occasionally lovingly referred to as "Mommy," was going to make it even shittier.

"Not now, my ass," she grumbled in response. "Trish just called saying that y'all had a situation. Shit was fucked up and that she was leaving," she continued. "What the hell is going on Josiah?" she demanded to know.

While she waited for a response, she walked barefoot across her luxurious kitchen, until she reached her six-burner, stainless steel gas stove. She reached down and carefully lifted the lid off the large pot she had on top. Letting the steam escape, she grabbed her large spoon off the nearby granite counter and stirred her soup. Despite living in Florida with year-round, warm weather, Lolita was still preparing her famous Carne Guisada. Her children and grandchildren loved her Puerto Rican Beef stew, so she cooked it whenever they requested it. She didn't give a damn if it was nine degrees or ninety.

Josiah took a few seconds to respond. "We had a few issues. Nothing that can't be managed. I can't talk about it right now but---"

"Get your ass on the next flight so you can talk about it!" she demanded as she replaced the lid back on top of her pot.

Her beige, silk night-gown flowed loosely around her tall, lean frame as she spun her body around and prepared to walk out. Lolita was a very regal woman. Her presence commanded respect and that is exactly what she got. It was justly due since she was the late girlfriend and partner of the slain, Puerto Rican drug runner, Luis Bonilla. Together they ran drugs from Puerto Rico to the United States for a well-known crime family. For years, they had a successful run, with Lolita being the more cautious of the two. When Lolita began having babies, Luis demanded that she begin sitting out the runs, and that he go alone. He would eventually be caught, detained, and handed down a lengthy prison sentence. He would later be killed in prison during a gang riot. Lolita always lived with guilt. She knew if she had been there with him during that dreadful run, then he wouldn't have been caught. She would later relocate her children from Florida to Delaware for a fresh start. With her daughter and grandchildren, she would later return to the South for a slow-paced life in the sun.

Josiah on the other hand; was a different story. He was a lot like his father: ambitious and interested in the drug game. However, Josiah wasn't interested in just running drugs; he wanted to distribute them. With his mother's guidance and connections, he was instantly plugged in. Unfortunately for Josiah, it was just that: his mother's connections. Because she knew the plug personally, she felt that she had to know every detail of Josiah's business dealing. If she didn't approve of something, she could literally shut it down. And she did just that without hesitation. It wasn't that Lolita wanted to control what Josiah did; she wanted to protect him. She wanted to make sure he didn't slip up. She couldn't bear to see her baby boy stuffed in a jail cell, or worse: dead. She wouldn't allow it.

"Okay, I have to handle a few things, but I'll be there by tomorrow," Josiah responded respectfully, with as much patience as he could muster up.

"Good. We would all love to see you anyway. It's been several weeks. We miss you," Lolita admitted, softening up her tone. She had a way of being stern, yet still very loving and gentle. Her children were her weakness, but she did her best to keep that from dictating how she communicated with them.

"I miss you all too. Let everyone know I'll be there soon," Josiah replied, before saying goodbye and hanging up.

He sat his phone down in the seat beside him and stared off at nothing. He knew that Trish was heading to Florida and would tell his mother what was going on before he got the chance to.

He would have no choice but to be completely honest with her. There was no doubt in his mind that she would be calling for him to get out the game. Knowing his mother, she would even go as far as halting his ability to even get a new shipment.

৩৯৩

JOSIAH WATCHED as Trish quickly walked out of the bakery, clutching her purse and holding a big brown box in her hand. She scurried down the block towards the back of the building where her car was parked in a small gravel lot. He wondered where she was in a rush to. The man in him wanted to jump out and help her carry her things to the car but judging by her tightly balled lips that were curled up into a nasty scowl, she would probably decline the help. Josiah knew that Trish had every right to be upset with him. She loved him, and although she'd been unhappy just being his business partner, she settled for the role anyway just to be close to him. A part of Trish felt like she was being led on, although Josiah didn't necessarily agree with that. He flat out didn't want her, and he did his best to make that clear; however, Trish was one of those women that felt that she could change his mind over time by being there for him and being loyal. That simply wasn't the case.

"Trish!" Josiah quickly turned on his car, rolled the window and called out from the car.

Recognizing the voice, she snapped her head around and kept walking towards her car. When she finally got to it, she unlocked the doors, pushed in her boxes and peeled out of the parking lot. She had a last-minute flight to Florida that she was trying to hurry to. She'd return for her things later, but for now, she had to get the hell away from Wilmington *and* Josiah.

Josiah watched as she sped out of the parking lot and away from the bakery like she was being chased by the police. He shook his head and proceeded to look ahead. He had enough shit going on in his head. He wasn't about to give his energy to

Trish's temper tantrum. Instead, Josiah buckled his seat belt up to head home. Before he fired up the engine, something told him to check and make sure Trish locked up. He jumped out of his car and walked to the entrance of his store. He pulled at the handle of the front door. Just as he suspected; she'd left it unlocked. Josiah returned to his car and pulled the keys out of the ignition so he could use them to lock up. He started with the front door, side door, and finally the back door. Once all doors were secured, he returned to the front to leave. Just as he was coming up, he stumbled almost directly into two, Caucasian police officers. Josiah immediately recognized them as federal police officers; DEA to be exact. He'd had his run in with them in the past, and he damn sure didn't want to be reacquainted with them.

"How you doing? I'm Officer Cooper. He pointed to his right where his partner stood right beside him. "This is Officer Daniels. We're with the ---"

"I know who you're with, and I wanna stop you before you get started." Josiah immediately cut them off. He wasn't answering shit!

"Hold up," Officer Daniels started, raising his hand in the air to object. "We just wanted to ask you a few questions," he continued. Josiah assumed he would be the quieter of the two, but he thought wrong. You could never tell with the FEDS; and frankly, Josiah didn't have the time nor the patience to play guessing games. Besides, he didn't want to hear shit they had to say, nor did he have shit to say to them.

"With all due respect, I don't care what you want to ask. I'm leaving and if you want to speak with me ... get a warrant. When you do, you can speak directly with my lawyer."

Josiah walked off and left the two officers standing in front of the building. He immediately jumped in his car, sparked it up, and got the fuck out of there. As he drove down the city street, he made an immediate decision that he was getting the hell out of Wilmington.

3

Asia's prior day had been nothing short of hectic from running around non-stop, while thoughts of Josiah had kept her restless and up all night. It was weird for her to be preparing for Mitch to come home, while another man was on her mind the whole time. Her thoughts instantly drifted to Josiah. She hated that she had made him feel the way she did. She cared for him so much, yet a cowardly part of her had surfaced. She was still wrestling with the idea of whether to tell Mitch about them. She tossed and turned all night but still couldn't find the courage to stand in front of Mitch and tell him that she had been sleeping with his friend. And not only had she been sleeping with him: she loved him.

Despite being up most of the night before, Asia still managed to crawl out of bed first thing in the morning to go meet Mitch's lawyer at the bank. Like he'd promised, Josiah had wired her fifty-thousand-dollars the day before. While she pushed her Mercedes through the early morning traffic, she smacked her teeth at the snail-like pace they seemed to be moving at. Hasan was with Mitch's mother Juanita, who was also already up preparing for the day's festivities. Although Mitch wanted his arrival to be a surprise; Asia decided that she would turn the tables, and they would surprise him instead. Juanita had called every family member in the city and was planning a welcome home party for her boy. Even if he didn't win the second trial, they planned to make each day that he was home count.

After driving for over forty-five minutes, Asia finally arrived. She parked her truck into the parking lot of the bank and waited until she saw his lawyer Simon pull up. After greeting one another, they walked into the bank together, so Asia could withdraw the cash. To save time, Simon was going to be the one to post Mitch's bail, while Asia took the lengthy drive to pick him up. He'd been waiting long enough to get out, so they didn't want him to have to wait any longer than he had to since the day had come.

Once Asia passed the money over, she left the bank and immediately began her journey to get Mitch. So many emotions were running through her during the drive. Excitement, disbelief, and shock. She was simply in awe. While those emotions swirled through her body, the moment also felt bitter-sweet. She still didn't know what to do, and so far, she hadn't done anything. She shook the thoughts of dismay and confusion and decided to focus on the road. Her favorite saying played in her head: *let the chips fall where they may.*

❦

SEVERAL HOURS LATER, Asia was so excited that she couldn't help but break out into a full-fledged sprint when she saw Mitch's fine ass walk out the cloudy glass, double-doors of the prison that he'd been held at for the past two years. He had a bright smile etched across his face, and he was clutching a plastic bag that likely contained his belongings in his right hand. He'd only brought out the bare minimum. The bigger items he'd accumulated during his stay, like his television; he'd left to various people.

"I can't believe this shit! I'm fuckin' free!" he yelled as he beamed brightly.

Mitch couldn't help but keep looking around to make sure things were truly happening and it was all real. While he took it all in, he extended his arms and caught Asia in them as she rushed into his chest; her hair blowing back from the early fall breeze. As soon as she reached him, she gripped him up in a tight bear hug. Tears stung Asia's eyes, threatening to ruin her perfectly made-up face. Despite that, she let them fall freely. She was so happy that she didn't want to let go.

"Your home!" Asia cried, reinforcing what he'd already said. It was if she still couldn't believe it herself. Mitch had fought hard to get an appeal. Even when no one else believed, he did. With her face still buried in the center of Mitch's chest, she continued to let the tears of joy fall. Her feet were now slightly off the ground from Mitch lifting her off them and swinging her around in a colorfully happy embrace.

"Let me look at you," he said, releasing her at the same time she let her bear-like grip go from his body.

He couldn't help but smile in awe at what he saw. Milk and water had done her body a whole lot of good. That ass was still thick, her skin was flawless, and her thick, natural hair was pressed to silky perfection and now hung nearly to the center of her back.

"You look good as shit!" he grinned happily, his eyes soaking up as much of her beauty as he could.

"Thank you," Asia replied, while smiling and blushingly looking away. Although she knew she was beautiful, she was still slightly embarrassed at the attention. Mitch had always been expressive in his appreciation for her appearance. Despite her discomfort, he continued to stare at her intensely. It was something about the way he looked at her now. The passion; the intensity. She had no doubt in her mind that he still loved her just as much now, as he did before.

Asia had no idea, but Mitch put her on a pedestal. Even though she had a relationship with another nigga while he was down, she still stood beside him. It didn't matter to her that he had a shitload of years on his head. She still rocked with him; even if it was just as a friend, providing mental and financial support. Mitch knew that she would never understand the gratitude that he felt towards her. He could say it repeatedly, but there was no way he could express his appreciation, other than simply showing it.

"You ready to get the hell up out of here?" she asked, wiping away her tears.

She didn't bother to wait for a reply. She began walking away from the building and towards the parking lot. Mitch followed closely behind her while he took in deep breaths of the country air.

"*That's you?*" he asked in awe, as Asia stopped behind her ninja-black, new-model Mercedes Benz GLB250 that Josiah had recently purchased her.

"Yeah. Get in. I want to get you as far away from this place as possible," she replied, quickly changing the subject.

She didn't want Mitch asking her a million questions about her new car. The last he knew; she had a BMW that Waleek had bought her. Asia hated lying, because she was no good at it. Actually; she was the worst liar ever. So, instead of telling a lie, she'd rather change the subject to avoid having to.

They both hopped in and snapped their seatbelts in place before Asia backed out and rolled out of the parking lot. The rich smell of leather poured into Mitch's nostrils, while he sunk his body into the plush seats and got comfortable. He glanced over at Asia as she concentrated on the road. He couldn't help but admire the woman that she had become since he had been gone. Her resiliency had helped her blossom tremendously. Gone was the helpless young girl that he foolishly left behind on her own. In her place was a beautiful young woman. He had no doubt that she would be successful.

"Where we headed?" Mitch asked, while he stared out the window and took in the tall, lush, green trees and mountainous terrain around them. Asia hadn't turned on the radio or set any music to play. She instead left it off. She figured Mitch would appreciate the quiet drive back into the busy, bustling city he had left.

Asia briefly took her eyes off the road and looked at Mitch. The sight of him nearly made her heart melt. He had changed so much. His body was broader, tighter, and a lot more fit. His beard was even darker and fuller. Most men went to prison and due to stress, returned home with their hair thinning, and damn near bald. Not Mitch. His fine ass had come home looking like a full-course meal. God had always been good to her when it came to sending eye-candy. Mitch, Waleek, and Josiah were all God's finest looking creatures. She glanced back towards the road.

"You'll see ... You just be patient," she replied quietly. "All that matters is that you're a free man. So, sit back, relax, and enjoy the ride."

Mitch didn't bother to reply. It didn't matter where they were headed anyway. Any place was better than where he'd just come from. He just wanted to go home with Asia, see his son, and go back to how things once were.

❃

"DAMN," Mitch said in awe. He had just stepped foot inside of Asia's new condo and he was impressed. He expected it to be nice, but he wasn't expecting it to be *this* nice.

When he was home, he and Asia had lived in an upscale apartment complex, but it didn't compare to the spot he was standing in. Although she hadn't been living there long, she'd already begun putting her personal touches on the spot. With Josiah's money, she had the previous carpets pulled up and replaced with fabric that was plusher and more luxurious. That was one of the very first things Mitch had noticed when he walked in. When they got to the door, he already knew without her having to say; he needed to take off his shoes. As soon as he sunk his feet into the thick carpet, he knew that it was no cheap shit.

"This is nice! I see you on yo' shit," he said as he walked around and continued to admire everything she had done with the place.

Asia had always had impeccable taste. The living room was shabby, chic. The look was crisp and clean, with a blue and white color scheme; while patterned pillows and furry throws made the décor pop.

"Thanks," Asia replied with a smile. She was glad that he liked it. As he walked around, she remembered she had something for him.

"Oh! I got you something."

Mitch's face lit up. He didn't know what she got him; nor did he even care. He was just happy to be out. Anything in addition to that was beyond appreciated.

Asia motioned for him to follow her to the back of the condo. He assumed whatever she had for him would be in her room; however, he thought wrong. He followed her into what appeared to be a guest room. The space was too basic to be where she slept. It was minimally decorated, consisting of merely a full-size bed and a shag rug.

"I got you some clothes to wear!"

She pointed over to the bed happily. Sitting on top of the perfectly made full-size bed was a bag from the Gucci store. There was also a tan Timberland box beside it. Mitch was thankful and moved by the gesture. Asia knew his taste and knew exactly how he liked to lay his clothes. However, he was puzzled as to why she'd brought him in the guest room.

"Fuck is this? The guest room?" he blurted out, glancing from

Asia to the gifts on the bed. He walked over and began digging in the bags.

Asia could sense the immediate attitude; however, she didn't really care. He would get over it. "Do you like your stuff?" she asked, ignoring the question. His ass was going to say thank you before she answered anything.

"Hell yeah. Thank you. A nigga definitely appreciates it," he responded graciously.

He began pulling out the clothes from the bags. He held them up and pretended to admire the details. He didn't want to seem ungrateful by disregarding the gifts, but he wasn't trying to talk about no damn clothes either.

"I'm sleeping in here?" he asked., while suddenly laying the clothes down on the bed. He looked around. His face now unintentionally sour.

"Yeah, for now," Asia replied.

Mitch chuckled a little; tilting his head back while he laughed as if he were tickled by something.

"What's funny?" she asked.

"You," he replied. "I'm trying to figure out why I'm sleeping in the guest room and not with you?" he replied, not missing a beat. "It just sounds nutty as shit," he added.

Mitch was one of those people that wore their emotions on their face. While he waited for her response, he stood stiff and eyed her suspiciously.

"Because that's where I'd prefer you sleep right now ... That's where I feel comfortable that you sleep right now."

She shrugged him off after the reply and proceeded to head out the room. She wanted him to go ahead and switch his clothes so they could head out. She also wanted him to cease with the questions.

"Why?" he asked before she could get fully out of the room.

The question stopped her in her tracks. Asia had been wrestling with how she would answer it all night and morning. She wasn't ready to tell him she was with Josiah; however, she didn't feel right sharing her bed with Mitch right away. It was the same bed that she shared with Josiah the night before. It also happened to be a bed in the house that Josiah had bought for her. She loved Josiah; and frankly, the situation was already bad. She didn't want to make it even worse by continuously adding to the disrespect. *What she felt was disrespect anyway*. To be completely honest, she didn't mind having sex with Josiah or Mitch since she didn't mind being in a relationship with either of the two men. Both of them were good to her and she loved them. However, she wasn't a hoe, and she wasn't about to bed hop between the two. She had to figure out a way to admit to her wrongdoings and clean up the mess she helped create --- respectfully.

"It's just complicated right now," she replied in a huff, finally responding to Mitch's question after standing there quietly for a minute. "To be honest, I didn't know you were coming home. I didn't expect you to come home."

She turned around to face him while she spoke.

"This is all a lot to digest for me. You've been gone for two years and I'd be lying if I said I wasn't seeing someone else recently."

She swallowed hard while she waited for Mitch's response.

"I respect that," he said softly.

Mitch was a realist. Females got lonely and Asia was no different. Although it was something that he chose not to think of when he was in jail; actually, it was something that he liked to push to the rear of his mind. However, he was no fool and deep down he knew that Asia was fuckin' someone.

"So ... Is it serious? I mean ... because I expected to come home to a family," he admitted. "The family that I called myself taking care of, even though I was down," he added

Asia grew instantly irritated. "Mitch, I know that you looked out for us. I didn't ask you to do none of that, although it was very much appreciated. But ... I do want to remind you that you felt the need to do that."

"I'm not saying it *like that*," he said, smacking his teeth and frowning.

"Well, how you saying it?" Asia threw her hand up on her hip angrily. She wasn't about to let Mitch sit in her face and make it seem like she owed him something because he had been looking out for them financially for the last three or four months. She was the same person who held him down when the money ran out, while asking for nothing in return.

"Look ... I understand. You got needs. We all do. All I'm asking is, if it's not that serious, can you dead that shit and we continue to be a family how we were before."

Mitch wasn't about to play games, nor go back and forth with Asia. He wanted to be with her and his son. He'd give her time to decide, but he needed her to make a choice. He didn't go through all that he went through to get an appeal, only to get out and be without them.

"Okay," she replied simply, before walking out the room. Mitch had spoken his peace and she wasn't about to go back and forth with him. The day was special; he'd just been released, and they were going to enjoy it.

"And change those clothes," she called out once she got into the living room. "We bout to go somewhere special!"

After hearing him reply in agreement, she walked into the kitchen and poured herself a drink. She was glad that she was able to get out of the room before Mitch asked her anything else. It was hard enough admitting that the bit of information she just did. While she sipped strawberry lemonade from her glass, her mind went back and forth between Mitch and Josiah. She still didn't know what the fuck to do. Both were sexy as hell. They both were good men and good providers. They both loved her. She was so confused. She didn't want to betray Mitch, and she didn't want to hurt Josiah. It was fucked up she had to even make a stupid choice like this. *Lord, why can't I just have them both*, she said to herself. *If only life was that good*. She wished Mitch had gotten out before she'd even met Josiah and while she was still with Waleek. If that had been the case, then she would have had no problem kicking his black ass to the curb and moving forward with her baby-father. That just wasn't the case with Josiah. They stood on leveled ground, with Josiah possibly standing a little higher.

4

It's really been two years, Mitch thought to himself, as he unbuckled his seatbelt, got out of Asia's car and looked up and down the block that his mother had resided on for most of his adult life. West Oak lane was a neighborhood that the lower-middle class resided in. Clusters of beautiful brick rowhomes; well-kept patches of grassy lawn; small areas with cemented decks and patio furniture; the street was still just as quiet and beautiful like he remembered.

Mitch seemed to wear a permanent smile as he jogged up the six steps that led to his mother's front door. He knew she was going to be surprised when she saw who it was tapping at her door. He pulled back the white, steel-made storm door, and after a few knocks, he waited patiently for her to answer. Asia stood behind him quietly. After a few seconds he heard the patter of feet running to the door, and then it abruptly swung open.

"Surprise!" a large group screamed out, startling him. He didn't have time to react before his mother rushed into his arms and tackled him. She slung her arms around his neck and with tears in her eyes began planting kisses all over his face.

"Mitch!!" she screamed, her voice, trembling with emotion.

He returned her embrace and was instantly swarmed by all the people who had shown up at his mother's home to surprise him. Helium-filled, welcome home balloons floated to the ceiling; while aunts, uncles, nieces, nephews and cousins surrounded him from all angles of the small living space. Some stood quietly, some clapped, some wiped tears from their eyes, and some just held their hands against their mouth in amazement. No one had expected to see him home for the next twenty-years; so, to them it was like seeing a ghost.

When Juanita, Mitch's mom, finally let go of her son, she stood and just held his face. She was so happy to see him. Asia quietly eased alongside of him, smiled and mouthed "*surprise.*" All he could do was shake his head in amazement. He hadn't seen it coming. In the midst of his excitement, Mitch realized that someone very important was missing. He scanned the house and didn't hear him, or see him.

"Where's my son?" he asked, glancing from his mother to Asia, who was standing at his side.

"He's upstairs in my room sleep," she said. "Go up there and wake him up. He'll be just fine. Then get yo' butt back down here and get some of this food we got in here for you. I know you haven't eaten good in two years! We got everything!" she yelled.

Asia laughed and shook her head. Juanita had always been loud. She was even louder since her boy had entered her door after being gone for several years. She was so excited that Mitch was home, that she didn't even notice how drastically her volume had increased. Still standing in the living room, Asia glanced in the dining room. The large cherry-wood table was filled with foil-covered pans of food. There were several large bottles of mid-shelf liquor and a couple cases of beers. She looked for a place to sit but couldn't find one. The house was packed and there wasn't even an inch of space left on the pink, vintage couches that sat in Juanita's living room. She had the set for years, as they were given to her by her own mother. She'd had them restored years back and although small, they were still in immaculate condition. After saying "excuse me" a few times, Asia headed into the kitchen to make Mitch a plate. She knew his mother had probably already done it, but she still felt like it wouldn't be right if she didn't attempt. Asia finally managed to make it to the sink, where she proceeded to turn the water on and wash her hands.

"You fixin' something to eat?" Juanita asked, creeping up behind Asia unexpectedly.

"Yeah, for Mitch," she replied. She grabbed the roll of paper towels that stood on the counter and tore off a few sheets to dry her hands. "I'm not hungry just yet. I just ate, not too long ago."

"Oh, okay honey. Well, I done already made my boy a plate. It's in the warmer ... Actually ... it isn't a plate. It's more like a pan. Gon' ahead and grab it and give it to him. The sodas are in the refrigerator."

Waving her hand, she motioned for Asia to run along. Asia couldn't help but giggle at Juanita's bossiness. She'd always been that way. She didn't play any games when it came to her son. He was her only child, which didn't surprise Asia. She was actually more surprised that she'd had any children at all. Juanita was a borderline tomboy. She had a tapered cut, a raspy voice, and to put it mildly, was a little rough around the edges. She always kept it a hundred; and although she was far from perfect, she was solid.

Asia walked over to the stove, bent down and pulled open the warmer. She laughed when she saw the 13x9 pan that was filled to the brim and covered with foil. Mitch could eat, but not that damn much. Juanita was tripping. Asia went ahead and grabbed the oven mitts from the stove and proceeded to pull out the pan. Balancing it with her hands gripping both sides, she walked it over and placed it on the table; pushing over other pans to make space. Just as she was pulling the foil back to inspect the contents, Mitch walked up smiling wide with a still sleepy Hasan.

"Hey mama's baby," Asia cooed. She pushed off the oven mitts, reached over and rubbed the front of Hasan's head, wiping off the thin coat of sweat that was on the front of it.

"He got big as shit!" Mitch said as he looked around for a seat. Asia was already on it, spotting a few plastic, white ones stacked on top of each other in the corner. She pulled two from off the top of the pile and slid them across the hardwood floor to the table.

"Here. Sit down and eat. I'll take Hasan."

Mitch passed her their son and sat down to the table.

"I'm about to lay his butt right back down. Otherwise he's going to be cranky all day because he didn't give a proper nap."

"Put him back in Ma room. It's kind of loud down here anyway. I'll have plenty of time to hang out with my boy later anyway."

Asia nodded in agreement and headed back up the steps with a sleeping Hasan. Just as she was turning the corner in the living room to go up the steps, she heard a knock at the door. Asia wondered who else it could be. She didn't bother to try and open it; Hasan was heavy, and she wanted to hurry up and lay him back down. Before she made it halfway up the steps, someone in the living room opened the door. It was Mitch's right-hand man, Pop.

Pop was a short, dark-skinned cat that had an annoying voice and uncanny resemblance to the New York rapper Jadakiss. He too was also from South West Philly. He and Mitch had grown up together and had managed to remain friends as adults. She hadn't seen much of Pop since Mitch had got booked and sentenced. He did what he could for her and Hasan during Mitch's incarceration; however, Mitch had been his plug. Once he got booked, things dried up for Pop and he too felt the impact of his friend's absence.

Damn. Give him some time to get situated, was Asia's thoughts as she laid Hasan down on his back in his grandmother's room. She knew that Pop came by to pay his respects; but ultimately, she knew what he *really* wanted to talk about. Pop knew that Mitch had a connect while in prison, and he was simply trying to see how that was going to affect his movement on the outside. Pop was ready to make moves and she had no doubt that Mitch already was too.

5

Facing the wall inside his prison cell, Ethan cried silent tears. *I don't belong here,* he thought to himself. He pulled his thin gray, wool blanket up under his chin and trembled. He was scared to death. He wasn't just scared of where he was at, and the people he was around; he was also scared of what was going to happen to him. He'd been caught with a shitload of drugs and had no idea where they came from. Well, he had an idea, but without proof, they were his. He was the one that had been caught with them. As much as he plead with law enforcement, it all boiled down to one thing: help us and we help you. The problem was, he couldn't. So, here he was charged with federal drug trafficking. To make matters worse, he had a court-appointed attorney, and his job was no longer answering his calls. In fact, the number had been disconnected.

The first time, *and only time* his call was answered, he spoke to Trish. She assured him that although she didn't know what was going on, that she was there for him. Several days had passed, and they'd done nothing at all to assist him. According to the FEDS, Trish nor the other owner were cooperative. They refused to answer any questions and seemed to be letting Ethan take the fall for whatever illegal operation they had going on.

The feds knew that he wasn't a criminal; his bosses were. Unfortunately, they didn't have enough evidence to charge them, so they would have to settle for Ethan.

Lying in the fetal position on the top bunk, Ethan forced his eyes closed. He once thought he had it all figured out; now he was no longer certain what his future held for him. After laying still for several minutes, Ethan realized he wasn't going to get to sleep anytime soon. Instead, his mind was scrambling to come up with ways to get him out of the mess he was in. He reached up and dug in the front pocket of his federal-issued, cotton top. He dug out a piece of paper with ten digits scribbled on it. It was Trish's phone number. Before all of his belongings, including his phone, were confiscated, he retrieved the number and memorized it. Trish was the only connection he had to the source of his problems. She had the money to defend him, and contrary to what she was telling him; she also had knowledge of what the hell was going on. He was going to reach out to her and get to the bottom of things. That was the only option he had left.

⚜

"Wassup Pop?" Mitch beamed as he bounced to the door of his mother's home to greet his child-hood friend.

"Welcome home baby!" Pop smiled brightly, before throwing his arms open to briefly embrace Mitch. He hadn't seen him in several months; although he usually made sure to visit him at the prison whenever he could.

Pop already knew what Mitch had going on behind the prison walls. He was the one that orchestrated the cash pickups from the jail. Now that he was back on the streets, Mitch planned to fill him in completely on the move of a lifetime. One that he'd had in the works for a long time. He already had Josiah ready and in position; now all he had to do was prepare Pop.

"Feels good. Feels good," Mitch replied, as he let go of his friend. "You want something to eat? My mom cooked everything you can fuckin' imagine," he said, as he waved for Pop to follow him into the kitchen.

"Nah, I'm good right now. But, I will take a plate to go, if you can have somebody whip me up one real quick. I just stopped by to welcome you home and let you know I was around. Ready to get this money, so we can keep you here. You feel me?" he said, intentionally lowering his tone."

"Fuckin' right," Mitch agreed.

Just as Pop went to say something, Asia came back down-stairs. "Mitch, you got a message," she said. It was Josiah, but she didn't announce it. Nobody needed to know his business.

When Asia got to the bottom of the steps, she handed Mitch the phone. "Hey Pop," she said.

"Sup Asia," he replied lightly.

Asia didn't really have a relationship with any of Mitch's friends. He typically kept his "work" and his family separate. Pop was cool and she never had any issues with him. He seemed like a stand-up guy, and from what she gathered; he was fiercely loyal to Mitch. While Mitch was doing his thing in the prison, Pop brought her and Josiah money like clockwork. Mitch glanced down at the phone and read the text message from Josiah. *Change of plans. Meet me at the Airport. Delta departure area.* He wondered what was up that resulted in the change of plans.

"Babe, can you make Pop a plate to go real quick, please. Then we gotta run somewhere."

Asia didn't ask any questions. She scurried to the kitchen to make Pop's plate and then they were off.

❧ 6 ❧

sia did her best to push through the anxiety she felt as she drove her car through the departure area for Delta Airlines at the Philadelphia Airport. As she searched for a place to park, Mitch looked through the crowd in search of his friend Josiah. After less than a minute of searching, Mitch spotted him leaning up against the wall. Asia glanced at him and could tell the flight had been last minute. Josiah normally traveled light, but today he had nothing at all with him. Not even the small bag that usually contained his underclothes. She wondered what was going on that required him to leave so suddenly. Spotting a parking spot between two yellow cabs, she slowed to a stop to let Mitch out.

"I'm going to back into a parking space while you get out and talk," she said.

Mitch nodded and hopped out. She was about to tell him not to be all day, but she decided against it. A part of her hated to see Josiah leave anyway. She was truly thankful for any moment she got to lay her eyes on him. She knew that very soon; it was going to be a rare occurrence.

After finding a parking space, Asia watched discreetly as Josiah seemed to glide over to Mitch. He had a warm smile on his handsome face as they shook hands and then embraced for a brief, brotherly-like hug. She could tell that Mitch was grateful to have him as a friend. Grateful for everything he'd done for him. She glanced away and down into her lap as a sick feeling crept into her stomach. Anxiety, disappointment, and sadness overcame her all at once. Finally looking up, she glanced back over at Mitch and Josiah. Their expression had changed from jovial to serious. Something was up. She wondered what the hell it was.

She studied their faces intently to see if she could read their lips. When she realized she couldn't; she smacked her teeth. She knew Josiah would never mention their relationship but there was a small part in her that could never be too sure. She couldn't even trust her own mama, so she damn sure wasn't going to put all her trust in a nigga. When she glanced back over to them, she saw the two of them approaching her truck. She stared ahead as they hopped in. Mitch hopped in the front, while Josiah hopped in the back seat.

"Wassup Asia?" Josiah greeted her casually after the back door slammed shut behind him.

"Hey Josiah. How you been?" she asked glancing in his direction, before forcing her eyes away. If they had their way, they would have stared at his ass all day long. She did her best to sound normal and make conversation. She'd hate for Mitch to detect anything between the two.

"Been good," he replied.

"Everything okay?" she asked Mitch, redirecting her attention to him.

She had picked up his solemn demeanor as soon as he sat down beside her. While she waited for a response, she couldn't help but feel Josiah's eyes on the back of her head. He did his best to remain focused on business, but he couldn't help the jealous feelings that were creeping up on him. He quickly shook them off.

"I'm hoping," Mitch replied casually to Asia's question.

He stared ahead, while Josiah proceeded to fill him in on what was going on. He didn't say too much, since he had grown up being told to never let anyone know every little detail involving your business. The only person who had that luxury was his mother Lolita.

"I'm hoping I can ride this shit out. For now, I'm going to have to shut down shop. I can't make any moves. Especially not knowing if I'm under surveillance. I have no doubt that if I'm not already, then I will be soon. Everything stops. Even the bakery for now. I can't risk another FED case; especially if it puts Trish at risk."

As soon as the statement rolled off his tongue, Asia glanced in the rearview mirror and looked directly at Josiah. He caught the look she gave and met her gaze. He instantly spotted the jealousy in her face and for some reason, it gave him a sense of satisfaction.

Who the fuck is Trish? was her immediate thought. She had never heard the name before, and frankly, she wanted to know who the hell it was.

"She still in the city?" Mitch asked.

"Na. She flew back down South earlier," he replied.

Josiah already knew what Mitch was getting at. Trish knew a lot. Getting her far away so she could no longer be questioned was imperative. Josiah didn't bother disclosing that Trish had left willingly. He also didn't bother to mention that they weren't currently on the best of terms. That wouldn't have been a good look on any level. When he got to Florida, he planned to smooth things over with Trish. He didn't want there to be any bad blood between them. Josiah wasn't particularly worried. She was loyal to a fault; however, she still knew enough to bury him.

"Cool. You gotta do what you gotta do. Keep me posted."

"Bet ... Look, I gotta run. My flight leaves in about thirty-minutes. I'll hit you when I touch down and I'll let you know how things are looking as soon as I can." With those promises made, Josiah exited out of the vehicle and disappeared back into the crowd.

Once Josiah was no longer in sight, Asia started her car back up and slipped back into traffic to get them back into the city. Thoughts swirled through her head as she wondered what was going on. Whatever it was, she knew it was drug-related. She also knew it wasn't good. She was going to call Josiah later. She could easily get his flight information when they got back to the house. She just needed a minute to get away from Mitch.

While Asia was deep in thought, Mitch too had thoughts swirling through his head. Josiah was his connect and now could no longer supply him. Mitch knew he could find another supplier, but he didn't know if they could deliver on the level that Josiah did. He also had to find someone that he could trust. With his upcoming appeal ahead, he had to keep a steady flow of funds coming in. He didn't expect Asia to pay the monstrous legal fees he knew he would accumulate. Not only was she in the process of opening another daycare, she still had to cover all the household bills. With no way to keep the drugs flowing into the prison, Mitch knew his money was going to quickly dry up. His first day out, and he had already been backed into a corner. He had to make a move and make it soon.

❦ 7 ❦

J osiah tilt his head back against the lush, Delta passenger seat and made himself comfortable on his first-class flight from Philadelphia to Orlando. As the flight-attendant began her announcements through the loud speaker, he swiped through the messages on his phone. Like he had anticipated, he had several paragraph-length messages from Asia. He shook his head as he quickly read through them.. *The audacity of this broad*, were his thoughts after he finished.

Although Asia's initial text messages were apologies, the most recent ones were basically demanding to know who Trish was. She even accused of him of living a double life. Her jealous side was rearing its ugly, little head, and he didn't have time for it. He hadn't lied so he didn't really feel like he had to explain anything at all to her. All he had done was love her and her son. He'd done nothing but be there for her and Mitch; and this is what he wound up with: nothing. Josiah knew he wasn't perfect but he was good to those he fucked with. He didn't even bother responding to Asia's texts. Instead, he put his phone in airplane mode, stuffed it in his pocket and proceeded to stare out the window.

Josiah stared at the beautiful view as the plane elevated

higher and higher into the sky. As jealous and frustrated as he was, his thoughts still drifted back to Asia. What he was doing now, was exactly what he wanted for the both of them. To elevate as a couple. To sit on top of the world together. He didn't understand why he had such bad luck with women. Contrary to popular belief, it wasn't always easy for a rich ass hustler to find a good woman. Most of them were taken, damaged, or simply money hungry.

Josiah thought about his friendship with Mitch. He never had any intentions of crossing his friend. He'd acted selfishly and despite his reasoning, he knew he was wrong. He was going to fall back. Since he'd last saw them at the airport, Asia had been blowing his phone up with text messages and demands that they speak. He wanted to, but it wasn't a good look. Besides, he had other shit on his plate.

Trish was an emotional wreck, and he didn't know what the fuck was up with Ethan. Trish was right; he didn't know what Ethan knew. Assuming he knew nothing, wasn't good enough. He needed to be certain ... and he simply wasn't. He had been putting so much time and effort into Asia and supplying Mitch through the prison that he had neglected the bakery and all the people that he supplied through it. Now he was potentially fucked. He was going to do the best he could to right his wrongs with Trish, even if that meant putting up some big bread for Ethan's defense. He vowed to be a better man, since at the end of the day, he truly loved Trish. Although he wasn't in love with her. Until then, all he could do was sit back and see how everything would unfold.

8

"I gotta take care of some business," Mitch said as soon as Asia pulled up in front of his mother's house after returning from the airport. She immediately noticed Pop's burgundy Ford Taurus parked nearby. A frown spread across her face.

"Already?" she asked. "You literally just got home. What happened to spending time with ya son? I drove all that way to get you and bring you back, and you gonna take off with Pop?"

Mitch took a deep breath and then turned his body to face Asia.

"I plan to spend a lot of time with him and you. But there's been a change in plans so I gotta slide with Pop for a few. Just to line some shit up."

Asia smacked her teeth and peered out the window. *Some things never change*, she thought to herself. While she loved and respected Mitch, she hated that he always had a sense of urgency about everything. He was so strategic and always up to something. She could never tell with him. Since she'd met him, he'd always been a provider, but sometimes his methods scared her. She never knew what was going on in that handsome head of his.

"Why can't it wait?" she asked with a pout.

Mitch sighed. If only she knew what he did to make sure

they were good. Some things were better left untold and unsaid. He prided himself on being a hustler. He could turn lemons to lemonades; make something out of nothing. Even in the worst of situations, he would always come out on his feet. One of the lowest points of his life was leaving Asia and Hasan on the streets with nothing. All those nights in a jail cell, he vowed to fix it. He made a promise to himself to never let it happen again. So far, he'd kept that promise. So, although Asia never understood his logic right away; she always knew that he had her best interest in the end.

"I won't be long. I gotta sit down with my man for a little bit. Run over a few things, and then I'll get him to drop me off," Mitch finally responded.

"Okay," she grumbled.

There was no need going back and forth with him since she knew his mind was already made up. A part of Asia knew that their discussion was going to be about drugs. Mitch was out on bail, and she knew that he had to get things moving and get some money coming in. One thing about Mitch: he was a go-getter. She had no doubt that in very little time, he would be back like he never left. However, she didn't know if that was such a good thing.

"I love you, babe. And don't be mad," Mitch said, as he climbed out of the car. "I promise, I got y'all."

Asia watched him walk off and hop in Pop's car. "I don't doubt that," she said to herself as she watched them pull off and head to South West Philly.

Asia shook her head in dismay. *Josiah would never*, she thought. He hadn't even been home twelve hours and he was putting his family on pause. She damn near felt like she was downgrading. *Is this really what you want to put up with when you got a nigga that loves you to death?* she asked herself. Mitch had better get it together ... and fast.

❧ 9 ❧

It was dark when Asia arrived home with her son. They'd already eaten, so she quickly got him situated and used the time to also wind down. After putting away her things and peeking in on Hasan while he sat in his room and watched cartoons, Asia grabbed her cell phone out of her purse and went into her room to call Josiah. She'd been texting him since earlier that day. Needless to say, he hadn't returned any of her texts, nor bothered to call her back. Despite everything that she had going on, thoughts of Josiah clouded her brain. She hadn't even bothered to call her daycare to check on things and see if everything was running smoothly. She pushed the daycare to the back of her thoughts. She had confidence in her employees and was confident that they had everything under control. She had to get her personal life in order. She looked back down at her phone and tapped Josiah's name so her phone could redial him again.

Much to her surprise, it rang twice, and then he answered.

"Wassup?" he asked, in a nonchalant tone. He hadn't even bothered to say *hello*.

"You didn't see my messages?" Asia snapped with extra attitude. "You didn't see my calls?" she continued.

"I was on a flight," Josiah responded as if he didn't have time for anything she was saying.

"Why you acting so nasty?" she asked in disbelief. This attitude and behavior were all new to her. She didn't like it one bit.

Josiah laughed at her nerve. He had just got off a two-and-a-half-hour flight from Philadelphia and had only been in Florida for several hours. He only had a few missed calls and didn't have any voicemails. She'd just recently started calling him. Asia always left voicemails. He found it amusing that she was accusing him of acting a certain way, when it was really her who couldn't talk because she was around Mitch. Now ... since she was free, it was imperative that he pick up. *Get the fuck outta here*, he thought to himself. He loved Asia to pieces, but she was getting more ridiculous by the day. Although they occasionally disagreed, he wasn't used to conflict with her. It felt weird for them to be going back and forth.

"I'm not acting nasty. Hold on," he said abruptly.

He pulled the phone away from his ear and got up off the couch. He was at his mother's and his entire family was lurking close by, a few feet away from him. Needless to say; he wasn't on everyone's good side. It also didn't help that Trish had beat him there and made him out to be a self-absorbed, money hoarding, villain. As soon as Asia began attempting to blow up his phone, he started receiving dirty looks from his mother and sister. If he weren't mistaken, she had even mouthed for him to take his call outside. Even though he and Trish weren't together, his family still demanded respect for her. She was also staying there while she searched for a home and had just recently walked off to use the bathroom down the hall. After his mother's silent words, Josiah wanted to respond, but didn't. He wasn't fond of her asking him to take his conversation outside of a house that he fucking paid for. He had no plans of telling her that part of course, since Lolita wouldn't hesitate to bless the side of his face with her hand.

"Hello!" Asia rolled her eyes and paused for a response. "Hel-loooooo!" Asia repeated, yelling into the receiver.

"I asked you to hold on," Josiah mumbled.

He walked out of the living room and through the kitchen so he could access the giant deck that sat outside of it. He pushed through the door, and quietly shut it back so he could stand outside and talk privately.

"I want you to answer the question Josiah," Asia demanded. Why are you acting funny?"

"Come on, Asia. We're not children. I'm not acting funny. I'm distancing myself. You had me thinking that we were together. Better yet, we *were* together and then Mitch comes home, and it's *fuck me*. How am I supposed to feel? What am I supposed to do? I see you, and you act like you barely know a nigga."

"I was just trying to show Mitch respect," she started, but Josiah angrily cut her off.

"What the fuck about me," he growled angrily into the phone. "What the fuck do you know about respect, huh?" he asked. "Everything he's asked me to do, I've done! I put him on, like he asked me. Helped him make moves, like he asked me. I looked out for his family, like he asked me ... What about Josiah, Asia? Why I feel like y'all just fuckin' used me?" he painfully admitted. As tough and as strong as he was, he couldn't help but feel hurt.

"Josiah, no one used you," she snapped; however, that was all she could say. She wasn't sure how to respond to anything else he had said.

In a sense, he was right. It did seem like he had gotten the shitty end of the stick. He had been there for both of them. Everything that Mitch had asked him to do, he'd done. She didn't dispute his feelings. She didn't doubt that he was hurt; however, she never expected things to unfold the way that they had. She didn't know what he wanted her to do.

"I don't want you to even think for a second that either of us did," Asia continued. "Mitch loves and respects you. He speaks highly of you. And you already know how I feel about you."

"And how's that?" Josiah countered.

Asia smacked her teeth. "You know I love you. If things were diff---"

Josiah immediately cut her off. "Fuck if things were different Asia!" He paced around the patio angrily; however, he lowered his voice after realizing that he had gotten unintentionally loud. "Things are what *we* say it is."

"That's not how life goes Josiah."

"Why not?" he asked. "Life is what we say it is. Life is nothing *but* choices. Those choices are up to you. Whatever the fuck you want; whatever the fuck you want to do; you can. As long as I'm around ... you know that," he reminded her.

"You know that you can do whatever you want. You can have whatever you want. If you say, *I choose you*, I will do whatever it takes. You can be on the first flight to me ... You can open up as many daycares as you want; anywhere you want. If you go to Mitch and tell him, he will understand. But if you hide it, it gets worse. But only *you* can make that choice. I won't force you."

Asia sat stiff and quiet for a few minutes. She wished it were that easy. Standing up from her seated position on her bed, she finally responded. "I --- I --- I want to, Josiah. But he's my son's father. I can't do that to him," she said. She loved Josiah, but she still loved Mitch. She couldn't make a choice right now. She didn't have the heart to.

"Okay," Josiah responded simply. As much as he loved Asia; he wasn't going to beg her ass. "That's your choice. Not mine."

"I'm sorry Josiah."

"No need to be. I do want you to know though ... our relationship stops here. My business is with Mitch, so there's no need for us to be in contact."

"What?" Asia gasped.

"The fuck you think it would be?" Josiah snapped in frustration.

"So, you're saying you don't want to have shit to do with me at all because of what I just said. Did it ever dawn on you that maybe I'm not comfortable making a choice because you have somebody else!" she accused. It wasn't the reason; however, it was the best excuse she could come up with at the moment.

Asia loved Josiah and she honestly didn't want it to end. Not their relationship or their conversation. Before she got off the phone with him, she had to know about this other woman he mentioned. After all, that was the reason behind her fury of calls. Who in the hell was Trish!

"Who's Trish?" she demanded to know.

While he paused, Asia walked out of her room and went and peeked on Hasan.

"Trish is my business partner. She's practically part of my family. She's been friends with my sister since they were freshmen in high school. We dated briefly but she's like a sister to me. I've kept it a hundred since I met you and you know that," Josiah explained.

He wasn't into games and he figured he would lay it all on the line. He'd done nothing but put her first. Even his business had come second to her, and look where it got him: unfocused and under investigation. Of course, he didn't blame Asia. Neglecting his business wasn't her fault. He loved Asia; however, he wanted her to realize that his love for her was starting to become his kryptonite.

"Yeah, *friend my ass*. If she was just a friend and is supposedly like family; how come I've never heard you mention her? Huh?" Josiah went to speak but Asia cut him off. "Did you fuck her? Yes or no?" she demanded to know.

"Asia, fuck Trish! I'm talking about us!" he exploded, as all his patience flew out the window.

Asia went to respond but Josiah didn't hear her because he was interrupted by Trish's voice from the patio door.

"So, that's what it is Josiah? Fuck me?" a teary-eyed Trish asked in disbelief, while Josiah's back was still turned.

Fuck, he thought to himself. Josiah had never heard her walk up. Although he tried to keep his voice down, his heated conversation with Asia caused his voice to carry. When Trish walked out of the bathroom and was about to head back into the living room, she couldn't but overhear him on the phone. Something told her that whoever Josiah was on the phone with, was the reason behind his distance.

"Asia, I gotta go. We'll talk about this later," he said before abruptly hanging up.

"Hello?" Asia said into the phone. She threw it down to the bed and it landed at her side. She wasn't even going to bother calling back.

⚜

JUDGING by the angry look on Trish's face; she was about to be a whole new situation. He quickly stuffed his phone deep down in his pocket and faced her. The look on her face, shattered his heart into a million pieces. He hated that he continued to be the cause of her pain.

"No, don't hang up. It's fuck me now huh?" Trish asked again, her voice cracking while she struggled to stay calm. "After I helped you build your fucking business. After ... helping you buy investment properties and stocks ... and helping you come up with ways to move drugs and not get caught! After helping you clean your fucking drug money!" she screamed. "It's fuck me! After all that?" Trish asked, inching closer to him, with a look in her eyes that was mixed with bewilderment and murder.

"Trish ..." Josiah growled. "You need to lower your fuckin' voice and calm the fuck down," he demanded. Although the house was huge, they still had neighbors that he didn't want hearing them. He hated to appear insensitive, but he didn't want the whole damn community all up in his business.

"No fuck you!" she hollered. "You don't get to tell me what to do anymore. You don't get to tell me to calm down. I've sacrificed so much for you," she trembled.

She did her best to hold back the sob that was begging to escape.

"I wanted to be a teacher," she cried. "But you convinced me to go to school and study business. *We can be a power couple*," she said, doing her best impersonation of him while mocking his words. "Remember that shit?" she asked.

She shook her head in disbelief. She couldn't believe how big of a fool she had been for him.

Tears began to stream down her brown, angelic face. Josiah looked away. He hated seeing her like that, especially because he knew that he was the sole reason for her hurt. He couldn't bear to look at the pain he caused. He told himself that he wasn't leading her on, but he was. Trish was an asset. She was smart, and he knew that she would help catapult him to the top. Josiah had helped her make almost every important decision in her adult life. In the end, he always persuaded her to make the choice that benefited him the most. Where she went to college; what she majored in; where she would make her home; even what jobs she decided to take, were all influenced by Josiah. He kept her close to him; all the while, having her act as his advisor and investor. In the end, he ended up rich, while she ended up heart-broken. Josiah went to speak, but before he could get his words out, he was met with a fury of slaps from a distraught Trish. As he restrained her, she proceeded to yell, kick, and scream, causing a scene.

"Calm the fuck down!" he yelled.

"Fuck you Josiah, let me go" she demanded.

"Not until you calm down!"

As she proceeded to struggle, his twin nieces appeared at the door. His sister and mother followed quickly behind while Josiah continued to try and subdue a grief-stricken Trish.

"Josiah! Let her go!" his sister demanded as she ran up to intervene. "I'll get her," she said, reaching out to grab her friend.

She knew how her friend felt about her brother. She had been telling her for years to let him go. She knew that one day, some other woman was going to capture her brother's heart and Trish was going to be left high and dry. Josiah wasn't really a player. To her, he didn't have the swag nor the patience. Maria knew at some point he was going to settle down. He'd been talking about it for years. As much as she knew Trish loved her brother; she knew the feelings weren't mutual.

While Maria attempted to intervene, Josiah finally released Trish. As he went to jump back away from her reach; she broke free from his sister's grasp, rushed towards him and slapped him again. Before Maria could grab her again, and before she could land another slap on Josiah, Lolita appeared. She quietly slid in the chaos. She usually stayed out of her children's arguments but the last few seconds did it for her. Enough was enough. Drawing her hand back, she landed one loud open hand against the side of Trish's face, causing her to gasp.

"Don't ever put your hands on my son again," she demanded firmly as she positioned herself between her and Josiah. With her back to Josiah she looked Trish directly in her eyes to speak to her.

"Now you're more than welcome to stay, but ----"

"Don't worry. I'm leaving," Trish said, still holding the side of her face.

She was still wide-eyed with shock. Everyone stood still, while she scurried off the patio and back into the house to gather her belongings.

"Ma, why'd you hit her?" Maria whined.

"She needs to keep her hands to her gotdamn self," she said flatly. She loved Trish, but she wouldn't tolerate her putting her hands on her son.

"And so do you," Maria grumbled quietly so no one could hear her. "I'm going to go check on her," she said, before taking off back into the house. "Go," she said, shooing her twins back inside when she got near the kitchen door.

She hated that they had witnessed that dysfunction. As they made their exit, Lolita wasted no time laying into Josiah.

"This shit is over for you two!" she said, as she inched close to her son with her finger wagging in his face. "I told you that wasn't going to end well. You can't use people for your own selfish gain Josiah. I raised you better than that," Lolita spat.

She glared at him angrily before walking off and taking a deep breath.

"Ma, I tried to tell her that I didn't want to be with her like *that*. She insisted on staying around. Thinking that I would change my mind. I love Trish, but not like *that*," he admitted.

"Just shut up Josiah! You don't know shit about love! You don't know shit at all. What you *should* know is the risk you take by playing these silly ass games. Do you know how dangerous a scorned woman is?" she asked.

She looked at him like he was a fool. Like he didn't have a clue.

"A scorned woman can bring you down in ways unimaginable."

Josiah sat quietly. As usual, his mother was right.

"Trish knows *everything* about you. About your business. She could bring you down in a matter of minutes," she argued, snapping her finger.

She stood and stared at her son, pausing intentionally for emphasis. "You need to fix this. Give her some space. But you need to apologize to her ... Now ... And then you'll apologize again tomorrow."

Lolita began walking towards the door that led to the kitchen.

"And get your affairs in order. Get rid of what you have and gather up everything else. No more shipments. I'm making the call now," she said, before disappearing through the door.

Josiah wasn't about to waste his time responding. Even if he wanted to respond; she wouldn't have given him a chance. Not only did he expect her decision; he respected it. When she called him to Florida, he knew she was going to pull the plug on his operation. He didn't blame her though. Josiah was human and he wasn't perfect. He didn't always make the best choices and sometimes he fucked up. He hated to admit it, but he needed Lolita's guidance. Now, more than ever.

❧ 10 ❧

Asia threw her phone down onto the bed. It landed at her side. After being dismissed by Josiah, she was still pissed. She wasn't going to bother calling him back. As much as she hated to acknowledge it; he was right. She was being selfish. She wasn't ready, nor willing to come clean to Mitch. She'd made her decision to carry her secret with her. She knew Josiah would never say a word; so, she didn't plan to either. As much as it pained her; the decision had been made.

Asia got up and walked out of her room. She stopped by her son's room and peeked on him again. He had fallen asleep in his toddler recliner. She carefully scooped him up and put him in bed. After laying him down and clicking off his light switch, she headed into the kitchen. After briefly rummaging through her cabinets, she found the bottle of Hennessey she was looking for. She poured herself a drink; however, it did nothing for the pain that she was trying to mask. She was mourning a loss. Although Josiah said they would talk later, she knew they wouldn't. Her inability to choose was in fact, a choice. It was simple. She couldn't have both of them.. Now she had to live with that choice. And boy, did it hurt.

With her cup in hand, Asia took a seat at the dining room

table she had just recently purchased. Taking a slow sip from her cup, she thought about all the changes and adjustments she would need to make. Even though Josiah had gifted her the house and car, she didn't feel comfortable keeping either since they were no longer together. She made up her mind to sell her car. Although its value had depreciated some, she knew she could still get a pretty penny for the well-kept luxury vehicle. She was going to also purchase another bed. Those were two things she could start working on right away, with the latter being more urgent. As far as her house ... that was going to have to wait. Thoughts about her condo, reminded her that her deed had recently come in the mail.

She got up and retrieved her mail from her kitchen counter, where she usually kept it. After rummaging through the small stack of envelopes, she found the one with her deed. After reading through it, she returned her mail back to the kitchen and sat back down. She looked around and couldn't help but feel a twinge of sadness. She hadn't been in the house long and she hated to leave it. However, she knew that eventually it was going to have to go.

Asia finished her drink and then got up to shower. She glanced at the clock and realized it was nearly midnight. She thought about calling Mitch and then changed her mind. She instead sent him a text message. He had already told her not to wait up. He had a key so he wouldn't have any issues getting in. It was his first night home so she wasn't going to trip, but she definitely was going to let him know that he wasn't about to make a habit of strolling up in her shit at all types of crazy hours. Feeling a bit buzzed, she headed to the bathroom and called it a night.

❧ 11 ☙

Mitch and Pop were parked on a busy block in South West Philly. Although they were deeply immersed in conversation, they still managed to carefully observe everything that was taking place close by. It was early fall, so although the days were still warm; at night, the temperature fell low enough for folks to still wear their jackets. While Pop smoked his blunt, Mitch noticed that not much had changed. Teenagers in hoodies still hustled the block; while scantily dressed girls still walked up and down them. Crackheads were in and out. Cars still stopped and went. The block was still a busy, gold-mine just like he remembered.

Mitch remembered being posted up on the same blocks, with nothing but a pack and a dream. A dream to get rich and get up out of the hood. And he did ... but greed kept him close by, and arrogance would be the reason he went to prison. Desperation would bring him back, and that's why he was there today. He was desperate and he knew that the quickest way to get back on his feet was to do what he was known for: flood the hood with drugs.

"I got a team of niggas lined up and ready. They just waiting on the call," Pop boasted. For the last hour, he was briefing Mitch on the team he had put together while he was away.

"But can they handle a large amount?" Mitch asked.

"Hell yeah. That's what they been trained and bred for," he said. "I been prepping them niggas since you told me you were working on the appeal," he admitted.

Pop was a loyal soldier. He and Mitch had been thick as thieves since they were youngsters. Mitch had always been a man of his word. If Mitch said it; Pop believed it. So, when Mitch told him to gather a team of loyal hustlers; that's exactly what he did. Every week when Pop spoke to Mitch, he talked about his appeal. Pop knew he believed in it; so he believed in it too. Luckily. Now that Mitch was back home; he knew it wouldn't be long before he and his team were back on top where they rightfully belonged.

"Good," Mitch replied. "I risked a lot for this shit," he continued.

"Facts. You definitely did," Pop nodded in agreement, while he continued to smoke.

He attempted to pass the blunt to Mitch, but he declined. Weed didn't help him think; it made him paranoid, so he didn't indulge in it.

"You usually don't bring nigga's around the fam," Pop continued.

He barely went around Asia and Hasan. However, in order for Mitch's plan to work properly, he had no choice but to introduce Josiah to Asia.

"Right. Nothing against you. You know you my nigga. I just ..." Mitch paused.

He wasn't perfect, and he knew that one day his dirt would come to light. Hell, he'd been doing dirt since he was a young boy. He never wanted any harm to come to Asia or Hasan because of the risks he took, or the lengths he'd gone, to get to where he once was.

"I don't want shit to ever happen to them. I live for 'em," he said simply.

"No doubt," Pop replied.

A part of Mitch was glad that Asia didn't know the gritty side of him. He knew she wouldn't like it. There were a lot of things she didn't know, and that was for her own good. A lot of things he would never tell her.

"How you feeling about shit?" Pop asked.

He knew his friend too well. Mitch had always been an upbeat, chatty-ass nigga. Before he was a hustler; he was a hoodlum --- a stickup kid. That had been the plan for Josiah. With Mitch's back against the wall, his grimy, survival instincts would kick in full force while he lay desperate in his jail cell. Now, that a little time had passed, Pop was hoping his friend wasn't getting cold feet.

"Shit is, what it is," Mitch replied coolly. "It's not like we gon' off the nigga. We just gon' take his shit," he said.

When Mitch met Josiah several years ago; he immediately saw a victim. A family-oriented, pretty-boy with no real ties to the streets. He knew a hood nigga when he saw one, and Josiah was no hood nigga. He was instead, a rich nigga. A rich nigga from Delaware who would need an ally from Philadelphia; especially while he was locked away in an unknown jail, in an unknown city.

Mitch's whole goal was to capitalize off the situation. He never intended for Josiah to become his friend; he was his come-up. Moves were moves, and money was money, and he had no doubt that Josiah had access to a lot of it. With his Spanish heritage and Florida ties, he knew that he had met a big dog. Either way, he knew that Josiah had more bread than he could ever imagine. He also had a weakness: his good heart. Josiah had a good heart and he was loyal. Mitch also learned that Josiah had a small circle that he'd seemingly do anything for. A circle so small ... they were essentially family. Most hustler' never saw the betrayal coming from within.

❦

I⊤ WAS the wee hours of the morning when Mitch finally stumbled through the door of Asia's condo. He wasn't high or drunk; he was tired. After securing the locks behind him, he kicked off his wheat brown Timberland's and sat them neatly by the door. Before he headed to his room, he dropped his keys on the dining room table. He noticed the glass and knew that Asia had been up drinking. She was usually very neat; however, she'd left a stack of papers messily strewn across the table.

Picking up the papers, he began going through them. Most of them were bills. He smiled when he saw that they were all paid up and current. Asia had grown and matured so much since he'd been gone. She was building a beautiful life for their son, and was also now handling responsibilities effortlessly. Josiah continued picking through the bills before he came upon what appeared to be a deed. He scanned through it curiously and for a brief minute, was thrown off. He thought Asia rented the condo that they were in. *How the hell did she get approved for a mortgage?* He thought to himself. She was only twenty-two and had no credit history. He didn't remember her saying anything about ever applying for one, or even owning a house? Something like that, he would have certainly remembered.

Mitch sat the deed down and then picked it back up and re-read it. *I'm tired as shit. Maybe I read it wrong*, he thought. After rescanning the letters contents, he realized he hadn't. There was no mortgage lender listed on the deed. He wasn't an expert on home ownership, but he distinctly remembered his mother's deed listing the name of the bank that had given her the loan.

Mitch glanced around the condo and noticed all the improvements and upgraded fixtures. For the first time ever, something didn't seem right. Something told him that Asia wasn't being completely truthful about how much money she took from Waleek. He pushed his chair back and got up from the table. As he made his way to the guest room to get ready for bed, he made a mental note to get some more information on Waleek. He wondered what else Asia was leaving out.

❧ 12 ❧

Several weeks had passed and Asia was actually starting to enjoy her new normal. Her new life now felt like her old life but upgraded. Before, her sole purpose was to be Mitch's girl and Hasan's mother. Now, she felt more like Mitch's partner. She had her own business and for the first time ever; she felt like she was truly accomplishing something.

"Mitch, are you going to come with me to see the building?" she called out from the kitchen.

It was early in the morning and she was making a light breakfast before they headed out for the day. Hasan was turning two in a few weeks, so he was now at the kitchen table in a booster seat, instead of in a high chair. While Asia waited for a response, she scooped some scrambled eggs out of the skillet and pushed them onto a small, toddler plate for Hasan to eat.

"Here you go, sweetheart. Eat your breakfast," she said to her smiling child. He was growing up so quickly and looking more like Mitch every day.

Asia continued rummaging through the kitchen. She threw some toast in the toaster and finished spooning the remaining eggs onto two plates for her and Mitch.

"Yeah, I'm coming," Mitch finally replied, after seemingly appearing from nowhere.

He had a towel draped around his lower body and beads of water were strewn about his chiseled chest. Asia glanced at him and quickly turned her head. *Whew child*, she thought to herself. Looking at him had her wanting to stick out her tongue and catch *everything* he was dripping. She shook the thoughts as she reached in the fridge and grabbed a carton of orange juice. Pouring herself a drink, she looked back at him. He knew what the fuck he was doing, and it wasn't the first time he'd done it.

"Well, you need to hurry and get dressed," Asia said, while Mitch bent down and assisted their son with his breakfast.

She loved how he was so attentive to him. That was one of the best qualities about him. He took care of those he loved and did his best to express it. There was nothing he wouldn't do for them. *I made the right choice*, she told herself. That's what she like to tell herself.

"Come on. Get dressed. Eat your breakfast and lets go. Hasan is fine. Plus, I told the agent ten o clock. I'm dropping Hasan off at the daycare first, and then we'll shoot over to check out the space."

Mitch wiped his son's mouth and stood straight. "Ok, boss," he laughed, before heading back to the guest room to get dressed.

❦

"I EITHER WANT the previous judgement thrown out, a modified sentence that includes time-served, or an acquittal at the new trial," Mitch huffed in aggravation as Asia navigated her new Audi Q7 down the rough city streets, in route to Germantown.

She had traded in her Benz several weeks ago, with Mitch persuading her to upgrade to an SUV. Things were taking off on the street, so he didn't mind throwing in the difference after the dealer gave her the value of her trade-in. He didn't mind pitching in. After all she'd done for him, he felt she deserved it.

"I know that," Mitch paused while he continued to listen to his lawyer talk and spew a bunch of legal terms over the phone.

"But isn't there something you can do to work that shit out?" he asked, his frustration beginning to peek through his tone.

Asia glanced to her side and shot Mitch a worried look. She could tell he was becoming frustrated. Every so often he would run his hand nervously through his thick beard. He always did that when he was nervous, agitated, or trying to keep his cool. She sent him a look of reassurance when he finally glanced in her direction.

"Yeah, alright," Mitch responded dryly before hanging up the phone. Gripping it tightly, he stared ahead out of the window.

"You good?" Asia asked with concern, while doing her best to focus on the busy streets and traffic around her.

"Yeah ... Some shit he sayin' is cool ... but ... some of that other shit, I'm not rocking with."

"Like?" Asia urged him to continue.

"Well, he's saying the appeal will probably take a few years. That's a good thing. You know Philly courts always backed up."

"Right. Which gives you time to cover all the expenses."

"Exactly. And it also stalls for time. So, I have more to spend with you and Hasan."

"Well, we not thinking like that. We can't focus on, *what if you go back*. We gotta hope for the best outcome."

"Yeah. But this nigga Simon basically can't guarantee me shit. There's a chance I could beat the new case ... but if I don't, they can hand me back the same sentence. Like, what the fuck am I paying this nigga over a hundred grand for?" he shook his head. "He should be able to guarantee me a lighter sentence if I do get found guilty a second time. Time served, *or something*. He keeps saying, *it doesn't work like that*. I don't want to hear that shit," he complained.

"It'll be okay, baby. Just stay positive like you always have, and try not to get frustrated. It'll work out," she said.

She reached out her hand and rubbed his thigh to comfort him. It was something she used to do years ago when he got frustrated. Mitch glanced over at Asia and a huge smile spread across his face. She had that effect.

"Girl ... Don't start nothing in here. You gon' wake up the beast," he laughed. "You know I haven't had none of that sugar in years," he joked.

He reached down and rubbed his crotch to get his dick under control. Asia and Mitch were still sleeping in separate rooms and had yet to be intimate. Mitch was doing his best to respect Asia's wishes, but it had been weeks since he came home, and he was ready to pin her ass down and drill her into the bed. He hadn't acted on his fantasies, but he knew they would be fulfilled very soon. Mitch knew that Asia was going to eventually give in. He knew that he was a good-looking nigga and with Asia's sexual appetite; it was only a matter of time.

She used to always tell him, *"God took his time with you."* He knew she wasn't a hoe and he understood why she insisted they take things slow. She didn't want to feel like she was hopping from nigga to nigga. But he knew that eventually, that wall she had up, was soon going to fall down. He was intentionally doing little shit like walking through the house with no shirt ... or just a towel. Judging by her body language; what he was doing, was working.

"Yeah. I don't want to wake *him* up," Asia laughed, in response to Mitch's joke while pulling her hand away.

A few minutes later they arrived on a business lined street in Germantown. She was looking for a new location so she could serve another black section of Philadelphia; one that she was familiar with. After touring the building with the agent, Asia decided that she was satisfied with the location and the size of the space. It was going to be a perfect second location. Her goal was to own a string of daycares through the city. She loved children and she wasn't sure about what else to invest in. She knew she would have other ideas as time went on, but for now; she was going to put her all into the daycares. All she wanted to do was take care of her son, make moves, and stay busy. It was amazing how her life had changed so much in a year and a half.

❧ 13 ❧

"Ninety-eight, ninety-nine, one hundred," Waleek grunted, as he pushed up his dark, sweat-drenched body and lowered it back down to the cement floor for the last time. He rose up quickly, but instead of standing, he sat on the floor with his back against the wall of the tiny cell. He inhaled big, deep breaths while he waited patiently for his heart rate to slow.

While he waited, Waleek pulled his sweaty t-shirt from against his body and attempted to pull it back and forth to fan himself. He'd been locked up nearly seven months and the only thing he could do was exercise. He was already physically fit on the streets, but after putting on some weight from all the carbs the jail served, he was now beef cut.

"What time is it?" he asked his cell-buddy Charles, who was laying with his back against his bunk, reading a book.

Charles was a white guy who had just gotten a life sentence. He was going to appeal it, but at first he needed to educate himself on the criminal justice system. Every chance he got; he checked out books from the law library. He was scheduled to be transferred to a state prison any day.

"Quarter of four," Charles replied, looking down at the watch that he somehow managed to sneak in. "They're 'bout to do count."

"Cool," Waleek said with a grunt, as he came up from his sitting position and stood to his feet.

He usually tried to exercise right before count, so as soon as they were finished and opened the door, he could go shower and hop on the phone. He called home often. If he didn't stay on his case; nobody would. He also had to make sure his mother, Juanita wasn't running through his money. The same house that she forced Asia out of; was the same house that she had recently been evicted from.

Since he'd been down, everyone was having financial problems. It made him especially nervous that someone with financial problems was handling *his* money. Luckily, Asia had taken care of his lawyer. She'd actually obtained him from one of the top firms in the city: Bernosky and Glassberg. David Glassberg was no joke, and was already hinting towards a dismissal. If only the court systems weren't so damn backed up in Philly. Waleek had been sitting seven months and still hadn't actually had his preliminary hearing. The first one had been postponed, which he had expected. However, he never expected it to be damn near six months for them to reschedule another one. Fortunately, he had a new hearing in a few weeks. With a lack of evidence, David was strongly anticipating the judge to dismiss the charges. The only two witnesses the prosecution had been relying on, had been uncooperative and now had gone missing in action.

After finding out that Muff had talked to the police, Waleek no longer trusted her to be put on the stand on his behalf. She wasn't the brightest star in the sky, and he knew it wouldn't take much for her to get rattled and say some dumb shit that would have him further up shit's creek.

"I PROMISE YOU, it's really not that bad Muff. You gon' be cool.

Just go in there to make yo' bread and go home," Kareema said, doing her best to encourage her friend, who wasn't feeling the fact that she was now a McDonald's employee. Muff would much rather be the girlfriend of a ballin' ass nigga.

"This shit is wack as fuck," Muff complained with her lip poked out.

She adjusted her nylon, multi-colored bow tie, tucked in her shirt, and then walked over and looked at herself in her door mirror. Just as she suspected; she looked nutty as shit in the dumb ass uniform. Muff smacked her teeth but decided to proceed to work. She was flat broke, and since Waleek got booked, she hadn't had any luck finding a nigga that had any real bread.

News traveled through the hood fast that she had talked to the police, resulting in Waleek getting charged up. There wasn't a nigga in Germantown that was willing to fuck with her on the serious tip. Especially not the type of nigga she was used to. Although hustlers admired a pretty face; that alone wasn't enough. They wanted someone who was also loyal and solid. One who wouldn't fold under pressure. Muff had proven that she didn't possess those qualities.

Muff needed money, and she needed it quickly and consistently. With her daughter getting bigger and needing new things daily, she had no choice but to get a job. With the help of her friend Kareema, who was a swing manager at a McDonalds on Dauphin in North Philly; Muff was able to get a job through her. It wasn't what she wanted to do, but beggars damn sure couldn't be chooser's.

"Why they got me starting on a damn Saturday?" Muff groaned.

"Girl ... I don't know. They ass backwards in there. All I told them was to make sure that you worked with me your first couple of weeks. I want to make sure that I'm the only one training you up in there. 'Cuz them bitches is dumb as hell in there."

Muff rolled her eyes. *How much fuckin' training can it possibly be to work at McDonalds*, she thought to herself. Muff took a deep breath but decided to fix her attitude. She could at least show some gratitude to Kareema for vouching for her so she could get the job so easily. She didn't even have to interview or anything.

"I'm ready," Muff said.

She grabbed her purse and headed out the door. Her mother was keeping her daughter until she could find a daycare within walking distance that would take her. No one was accepting kids in her daughter's age group, so she was forced to keep her home. Luckily, her mom wasn't doing shit anyway.

"Ya mom keeping Kayla?" Kareema asked. Kayla was Muff and Waleek's daughter. She was also Kareema's god-child.

"Yeah. Until I find a daycare. There's supposed to be a new one opening up about eight blocks away in a few weeks. They had some flyers up with the address at the welfare office. I can catch the bus or walk to it, if I need to."

"Hell yeah girl. That's the move," Kareema replied, following behind Muff as they made their way out the door and to her first day as a cashier at McDonald's.

❧ 14 ❧

Josiah had been on the phone with his lawyer for the past half hour, and for the life of him; he couldn't understand why he couldn't seem to just do what he asked.

"Tim, why can't you arrange for the lease termination and then liquidate the inventory too?" he asked.

Josiah was trying to make his transition out of Wilmington as simple as possible. He didn't want to return, but he had to get all of his equipment out. The bakery ovens alone, were worth thousands of dollars. He was already taking a huge hit by breaking his lease; the last thing he wanted to do, was lose even more money.

"Josiah, that's not in my job description buddy. Now, I got them to cut you some slack on paying the lease. Especially considering the fact that you had just re-signed it and were only one year in, on a five-year agreement," he added in his nasal tone. "I can't handle my regular case-load *and* try to liquidate inventory. *And* must I remind you that I'm a criminal lawyer, not a contract lawyer," he added.

Josiah sighed. "I know Tim, and I appreciate everything you've done for me. I'm gonna reach out to Trish and see if she can take care of it. Any word on Ethan?"

"Oh yeah. I went by there to see him. I thought Trish informed you?"

"Informed me of what?" Josiah asked.

He now had a slew of questions but figured he'd let Tim speak to see if he would answer them without him probing.

"Trish retained my firm for Ethan. I thought she advised you. I haven't assigned him a specific lawyer yet; I figured, I'd go by and speak with him first. I thought you two discussed this."

"No, we haven't, but I will definitely run it by her. I'll make plans to get up with you, and we'll talk about it as well," Josiah said, before ending the conversation.

He wished that Tim could tell him what was going on then, but Josiah already knew how the phone game went. Details over traceable phone lines were prohibited. He quickly sent Trish a text. They needed to talk. He needed to know what the hell she was up to.

A few minutes later, his phone began to ring and vibrate. It was Trish.

"Hey. You said you wanted to talk to me?" Trish asked.

A part of her was happy to hear from him, considering that she hadn't heard from him since the day his mother smacked her, and she stormed out. He'd called and texted her apologies; however, she hadn't heard from him since then. Trish decided she wasn't going to be the one to reach out this time. She wanted him to blow her phone up; but in typical Josiah fashion, he didn't.

"Yeah, what's going on with you sending Tim to visit Ethan?" he asked. He didn't feel like beating around the bush.

"I told him I would help him, and *unlike others*, I do my best to keep my word."

"Trish ..." Josiah felt his patience instantly diminish. "I know you want to help him, but you have to be smart. Assisting him is going to make us look guilty. It's going to put us under the radar."

"Josiah, *please*. We're already under the radar. Besides, having

Tim on top of things will keep us abreast on what's *really* going on. Wouldn't you prefer someone to handle the case that's going to look out for our best interest as well. Would you rather be blind or prepared?" she asked, not really expecting a response.

Josiah quickly thought about what she'd just said. She was right, but he still didn't like how she'd went behind his back and orchestrated it. He made a mental note to keep an eye on both of them. Trish and Tim went way back. They'd met in college. Trish was actually the one that had introduced him to Tim.

"Yeah, whatever," Josiah mumbled.

Trish already knew how he felt about the entire situation. He didn't want to leave Ethan high and dry; however, that seemed to be the safest method. Trish had no idea what lengths the FEDS would go, in order to build a case. Ethan was the only link they had to him. Tim had already told them the safest thing to do, was cut the link and lay low. Trish was doing the exact fucking opposite. Her conscience and desire to do the right thing, was going to send them further up shit's creek.

"We can't just leave him for dead Josiah. We have to help him."

"Well, throw his grandmother some money. Let her handle that shit."

"I tried contacting her, but she was borderline hysterical."

Trish remembered all too well the theatrical performance of Ethan's ailing grandmother. She was beyond upset and was hurling questions at Trish that she simply couldn't answer without incriminating herself and Josiah. She just wanted to do the right thing and get Ethan out of the mess he was in. The FEDS didn't have much of a case. It was only handed over to him because Ethan had been detained with such a large quantity. Trish had called in Tim to see if he could get Ethan off, based on a technicality. Either way, she couldn't sit back and allow another person to throw away their life for Josiah. She'd lost too many years behind him; she wasn't about to let Ethan do the same.

"Well, you let me handle it from here on out. I'll make sure

Ethan gets the proper representation without fuckin' us all over," he assured her.

"Okay, Josiah," Trish agreed.

The two hung up and Josiah went back to his thoughts. He didn't understand how one minute he was on top of the world, and then the next minute, everything was fucked up. He had to start making moves to get his life back on track.

❀

"DAMN, that's all you could get?" Pop asked in disappointment. He held up one of the carefully, plastic-wrapped bricks of cocaine and inspected them.

"That's it," Mitch said.

He stared out the tinted window of Asia's truck while Pop sat next to him in the passenger's seat.

"Damn. This isn't gon' tell them nigga's nothing. When you think you gon' find a connect. My team getting antsy. We done had them waiting, and now we spoon-feeding them."

"I know. I didn't expect this nigga to get tied up in some FED shit," Mitch replied, growing irritated by his misfortune. He can't move any work right now. My hands are tied until I can find a new connect," he said.

Josiah's sudden departure from the drug game thwarted his entire plan. The original plan was to cop from him for several months and then jack him. Now, neither part of his plan could be put into play. He had no idea how the hell he would be able to find a supplier that could bless him on the level that Josiah did. The best thing about dealing with Josiah was he didn't even have to pay for the work upfront if he didn't have to. He knew it was fucked up for even considering robbing him. But hey ... business was business. Josiah's misfortunes had saved his ass.

Silence fell over the car, as both men pondered over their next move. Weeks had passed and Mitch knew that Pop and his crew were frustrated. He'd made all kinds of promises but had

75

failed to deliver on any of them. It was disappointing for everyone. Pop's entire team was ready, the streets were scorching hot, and Mitch hardly had any product to give them. He knew he had to make a move. He couldn't sit around and wait on Josiah to miraculously bounce back. He needed a new connect.

"I'm going to have to find a new connect," Mitch said aloud to no one in particular.

"Facts," Pop mumbled. He didn't understand why Mitch was just realizing that. "I might be able to help you with that," Pop continued. "You been gone for a minute and a lot of nigga's who was getting it when you were home; aren't getting it like that anymore. There's only a few heavy hitters, but they only deal with certain people. Shit is crazy out here. I'm gon' hit up this nigga I know and see if he can supply you with what you're looking for."

"Bet," Mitch replied.

It wasn't like he had much choice. Josiah was officially out of commission and there weren't too many people he trusted when it came to the drug game. Pop was one that he did. Hopefully he would come through.

❧ 15 ❧

A pearly-white smile pressed across Waleek's face as he speed-walked away from the city jail. Earlier that day, he'd beat his murder charge because of no witnesses and lack of evidence. He was officially a free man again, and he was happy as hell. As soon as the word *dismissed* rolled out the judge's mouth, he couldn't contain himself. Hours had passed and it was now nighttime; however, Waleek didn't care. He was just happy to be free.

As Waleek made his way down the dark, vacant street, his lip trembled lightly from the bite of the crisp wind that struck against his body. Ignoring the chill, his eyes casually darted around in search of his ride. After a couple minutes of walking straight, he saw the headlight's of Muff's car approaching. She was the last person he wanted to see; however, his mother worked the night shift and he didn't have anyone reliable enough to pick him up. His thoughts quickly drifted to Asia. He had no doubt that she would have been waiting for him when he walked out the building. He stopped walking when Muff's car slowed to a stop beside him.

"Welcome home," Muff said, flashing a genuine smile as soon as Waleek opened the car door.

"Thank you. And thanks for coming to get me," he said, barely giving her a quick glance. She hadn't changed a bit. Long weave, long lashes, and a whole lot of lip gloss. From his brief scan, he could tell she had gotten extra dolled up for him; however, as beautiful as she was, he wasn't the least bit interested.

"Where to?" she asked, once Waleek closed the door and got comfortable in the passenger seat.

"Uhhh, you can take me to my aunt house."

Since his mother had lost the townhouse in the county, she'd been staying with his aunt in North Philly until she found a new place. As cramped as they were, he had no choice but to stay there. He wasn't tripping though; he knew he'd be back on his feet in no time.

"You know you can stay with Kayla and me at my mom's. She won't care," Muff offered. She prayed he took her up on the offer. Since his incarceration, they hadn't been on the greatest of terms. Muff understood the strain; however, she was hoping that would all change soon.

For a moment, Waleek almost cursed her out. He didn't really want shit to do with Muff. Her sorry, ghetto- ass was the reason he was cased up and single. He didn't want Muff; he wanted Asia back. Despite how Waleek felt, his stiff, pulsating dick reminded him that he hadn't been active in months. His baby mama wasn't shit; but she was one hell of a fuck. Like R. Kelly, *his mind was telling him no, but his body was telling him yes.* He figured it wouldn't hurt for him to spend one night.

"Alright bet. Good looking."

A mischievous smile appeared on Muff's face. Glancing at Waleek, she couldn't help but lick her lips. He had put on some weight and was finer than ever. She was going to go extra hard so he could forget about all the bullshit that he'd just went through behind her. Waleek had always been a sucker for her sexual performance. Muff didn't really want him back; she just wanted to be back in his pockets. Ever since she knew him; Waleek had always been a money maker. She figured if she had to play, she might as well choose the winning team.

⸎

THE NEXT MORNING, Waleek rolled over and yawned loudly while sunlight spilled into the room from the window. As he stretched and struggled to adjust his eyes, he heard Muff call out to him.

"Hey, I'm glad you're woke. Can you take Kayla to the daycare," she asked.

After an intense night of going several rounds with Waleek, Muff was now faced with reality. She had to hurry and get her ass to work. She rushed around the room quickly, searching for her belongings. Stopping and standing in a corner, she flipped through clothes in her laundry basket until she found a clean uniform top. The covers slid down Waleek's bare chest as he sat up in the bed. The sight of his exposed flesh almost threw Muff off for a minute.

"Where is it?" Waleek asked her for the second time.

"Not far. You can walk there."

She reached in her purse and dug out a card. "Here." She walked over and handed it to him. "The address is on there. I'm running late and I'm already on probation for time and attendance," she admitted.

Muff didn't really give a shit about her job at McDonald's, but she knew she needed it until she had another stream of income coming in.

"You good. I got her. I'll finish getting her ready and take her."

Waleek didn't mind. He hadn't seen his daughter in a while, and he figured he'd might as well get acquainted with the staff at the daycare she was attending since they would soon be seeing him on the regular.

After thanking him, Muff gave their daughter a kiss and scurried off to work.

"Guess it's just you and Daddy," Waleek said to his daughter, who was standing in the middle of the small room playing with a black, naked Barbie doll that looked like it had been struck by lightning. Waleek glanced at his daughter's hair and figured her and the doll must have been outside together when the bolt hit. Her hair was also standing nearly straight up. She had one sock on and a stained t-shirt. Waleek sighed and rolled his eyes. His daughter's appearance was a strong reminder to himself not to get caught up with Muff's tired ass. His immediate focus was to get back on his feet and then get Asia back.

An hour later, Waleek had his daughter cleaned up and fed. With the help of Muff's mother, he also had her hair neat, and in four, pinky-length ponytails. After a brief walk, with Kayla proudly leading the way, they were now approaching her daycare.

"Is this it?" he asked his baby girl, knowing full-well it was. She smiled and nodded. She couldn't wait for him to meet her teachers.

"Good. What's your teacher's name again?" he asked, as they walked into the small building.

"Miss Braya," she replied. "That's her right there," she pointed.

Waleek smiled at the woman who damn near broke her neck to get to the counter and greet him. It wasn't often that father's came into the center. Especially not ones fine like him. Waleek felt the women staring holes in him as he approached the counter to sign his daughter in.

"Hi. You must be Kayla's father?" Braya asked, extending her hand out for him to shake.

"Yep, that'd be me."

"Well, it's nice to meet you. I'm Braya, the lead teacher." She pointed to and named three other ladies that were spread amongst the room. This facility only goes up to five years old, so we all work with your daughter. She has her days, but she is a pretty good kid."

Just as he was about to respond, he stopped. For a moment, he wasn't sure whether to be happy, sad or angry. The woman that was approaching the counter once had his heart. She was also the woman that had taken his money and left him. It was Asia.

ASIA WANTED to bolt in the other direction when she saw Waleek standing at the counter. It wasn't often that eye-candy strolled into their doors. When this particular piece did appear, the girls had sent hushed whispers, insisting that she see. She now wished she had kept her hot ass in her office. Waleek looked like he had seen a ghost when their eyes met, and so did she. She didn't expect to see Waleek again. She didn't expect him to be out this soon; but nevertheless, he was. She wanted to turn around and run; maybe hide. As she approached the counter and glanced into Waleek's eyes, her fear went away. She expected to see hate, but she didn't. She could tell that he still cared for her. As much shit as he had put her through, it certainly was a shocker.

"Wassup Asia," Waleek said, after collecting his thoughts and losing the silly grin that was on his face.

"Hey," she said reluctantly. She looked down and noticed his daughter still by his side. "Good morning, Kayla. You can go ahead and have a seat with the rest of your group." Kayla wrapped her arms around her dad's leg and squeezed tight before taking off into the center to join her class for instruction.

"Can we talk?" His eyes were almost pleading with her. He had to get some things off his chest; ask her a few questions.

Asia glanced around to make sure no one was listening. She didn't want everyone in her business. "Yeah, Waleek, but we gotta make it quick," she huffed before walking outside.

Waleek followed closely behind. "So, what the fuck is up with you?" he asked, cutting to the chase.

Asia rolled her eyes and then responded. "Waleek, I don't have time for this. If you got something to ask me; well then ask me," she said impatiently.

"I just got one question. How the fuck you just up and leave a nigga at his lowest point?"

He knew the answer, but he had to ask. Like a typical hood nigga, it didn't matter how much wrong he had done. All that mattered was the pain caused by his girl leaving him while in jail.

"*Your lowest point*," she scoffed before continuing. "Typical of you to only think of yourself. Did you forget, it was also *my* lowest point. You cheated on me. Had me out here looking dumb as fuck. Then ... your mother throws me onto the fuckin' street with my son. And let's not talk about Muff being pregnant."

She had so much she could throw in his face. That was only some of the things he had done to her.

"Okay, okay, you got that," he admitted with a nod. "You deserved that one."

"Deserved what Waleek? What did I deserve? To walk away after being treated like shit?" she asked. "Or, I deserved half your money. Actually ... not even half. The first fifty thousand went to making sure you had one of the best lawyers in the city. How you think you standing here today? Any other bitch would have taken it all."

Waleek didn't bother to argue with her. She was right. Despite her taking some of his money, he'd wronged her ten times over. He didn't give a fuck about the money. He planned to get it back tenfold. He just wanted her back. Even though he felt like Asia had shitted on him, she still was undeniably a good woman.

"Look, Asia, fuck all that. Fuck the money." He threw his hands up. "Obviously, you did something right with it," he said, referring to the daycare. "How do we move forward? How do we get past this? I just want you back," he admitted.

Asia folded her arms across her chest and stood and stared at Waleek like he'd lost his mind.

"Nigga ... Have you fuckin' lost it?" she asked. "Why the fuck would I want you back? What ... So, I can let you dog me twice? Plus, my baby father is home."

Waleek instantly grew quiet. That quickly, his chances had shriveled down to zero percent. The circumstances had dramatically changed, and Asia no longer needed him.

"Oh yeah. That's probably the real reason you left," he glared at her.

"Whatever Waleek. You had been down well before he came home. I left yo' ass because of all the foul shit you did."

"Okay Asia damn! We get it. I fucked up," he said exasperated.

How many times you gon' say the shit? he thought. He knew he wasn't the best nigga, but she couldn't deny the fact that he had taken good care of her while they were together. She didn't want for anything. The least she could do was show a little appreciation.

"At least let me make it up to you," he continued. It wasn't in his nature to give up that easily.

Asia didn't understand what Waleek didn't get.

"Make it up to me?" she scoffed. "How about you make it up to me by leaving me alone. Better yet, make it up to yourself by staying out of jail and getting yourself together."

Before Waleek could respond, Asia walked off and headed back into the center. She was cold and she wasn't about to give Waleek's ass another precious minute of her time. She hadn't even let him plead his case. He stood angrily for a few seconds before continuing up the block. He had other shit to do. He wanted Asia but he also had to get back to his money. One thing about Waleek was he'd never been a sucker and he always got what he wanted. If Asia wanted to be difficult; he'd just have to stir the pot a little.

ॐ

LATER THAT EVENING, Asia explained what had happened to Mitch. Just like she suspected; he was pissed. While he ranted and raved, she stayed quiet.

"Why the fuck this nigga think he can pop up on some nut shit, like somebody owe him something?" he asked, sitting on the side of Asia's bed fuming. "You haven't talked to him in how long?" he pressed.

"I told you since he left. When his bum ass baby mama exposed him and said she was pregnant, I was done. I did what you told me. I paid for his lawyer and was out."

"Well we do know one thing ... *His* lawyer did his fuckin' job," he said sarcastically. *Now, if only mine would*, he thought to himself.

"Yeah," Asia replied timidly.

Mitch's eyes shifted back over to Asia in concern. "You scared of the nigga or something?"

He wondered if there was more that she wasn't telling him. He still hadn't asked her how she managed to pay cash for the condo that they were standing in. From what he'd heard, Waleek was no lightweight. He made his money by seizing and slinging out of trap houses. Mitch made his money differently. He was a weight man, who barely touched the little shit.

"It's not that I'm scared of him. Waleek is just persistent. With that persistency, comes drama."

"Yeah, and it also comes with hollow's too," he stated coldly.

Asia looked in Mitch's black eyes and believed that statement. He'd been to jail for murder, and Lord only knew what else he'd done, that he hadn't been to jail for. Everybody knew how he got down.

"You don't have shit to worry about. Just handle your business."

He paused for a few seconds. He knew what he was about to say was going to be a little controversial. It wasn't the moral thing to do either; however, it seemed to be the best thing to do. Asia's reaction would indicate how serious she was about keeping Waleek away.

"You know you gotta put the little girl out right," he said.

"What do you mean, *put her out?*" she asked puzzled.

"Put her the fuck out. She can't go there," he said with finality. "You want to keep the nigga away. Put her little ass out. You know I love kids and all, but in order for you to keep him and his bitch away, put her out. Either that, or I'm gon' fuck around and kill that nigga for fuckin' wit' you."

After that statement, he got up and walked out of the room. Her baby's father had spoken.

❧ 16 ❧

"**B**itch! You weak as fuck!" Muff yelled across the counter. It was first thing in the morning, and she was going off after learning her daughter Kayla had been expelled from the center for "constant lateness." It was all bullshit to her. She'd just been told that morning with no advance notice. She had to go to work and was now going to be late because she had to find childcare. Her irate behavior was intensified when she demanded to speak with the director of the facility. When Asia walked her ass from out the back, and she realized *she* was the owner; it was over for the civilities.

"Miss, I know you're upset, but we need you to calm down. We have policies in place, and in order to run our center, we have to enforce them," Braya tried to explain while being constantly cut off.

"Bitch fuck yo' policies! This don't got shit to do with a policy. My daughter was going here just fine until her father dropped her off a few days ago. That hating' ass hoe found out that was my child, and now she being petty!" she screamed.

Braya stepped back from the counter while Muff went off. She'd already handed her Kayla's belongings and had explained the policy several times. She'd even showed her the policy in writing and where she had signed in agreement. They kept accurate attendance logs and sure enough, Kayla was constantly late. Although Asia was her boss and friend, Braya didn't agree with what she was doing. Asia had briefed her on the situation with Waleek, even going as far as filling her in on Mitch's suggestions to get her out of the center. Braya hated how their daughter was being thrust in the middle but Asia was adamant it was the only way. Even after Braya tried relentlessly to talk her out of it; she wouldn't budge on her decision.

Asia emerged from the back of the center, holding her cell phone up in her hand. When Muff stormed in, she had regrettably entertained her for several minutes before going to grab her phone to call the police. She could make all the threats she wanted, but for now, Asia wanted her the fuck away from her place of business.

"I called the police. You need to leave. This is a place of business and we have children in here ---"

"Fuck these kids, bitch! You don't give a fuck about *mine*! Why should I care about anybody else's!"

She snatched the plastic bag off the counter that contained Kayla's sheet and change of clothes. She was going to leave, but only because the bitch was about to involve the law. She didn't fuck around with the police. However, their situation was far from over.

"I'll leave, but trust and believe, I'll see you around bitch," she threatened, before gripping Kayla's hand and storming out.

And I'm gon' fuck you up, Asia thought to herself. *Don't let that professional shit fool you hoe.*

"Everything is okay," Asia said, attempting to quickly restore the temporary loss of order. "Back to your spots," Asia said to a few of the toddlers that were lingering around after Muff had left. She turned to her right-hand. "Thank you Braya. And I'm sorry you had to deal with that."

"It's okay," she murmured. "What's next though?"

"She won't be back. She'll probably start some shit when or if I ever run into her. *Which I don't plan to*, she thought. "But she won't be back."

"Oh ... Is that how she always is?"

"Who Muff?" Asia scoffed. "Hell yeah girl. A fuckin' mess. Always talkin' shit and quick to fight. All I went through was drama with that nigga," she said, lowering her tone while she spoke to Braya at the counter. "As fine as Waleek is ... I wouldn't touch that nigga with a ten-foot pole."

"Damn," was all Braya could say to wrap up their conversation.

She hoped she didn't have to deal with that. She hadn't told Asia yet, but Waleek had slipped her his number. The same day Asia dissed him, he later returned to pick up his daughter Kayla. While he waited for her to come out, he couldn't help but notice that Braya was checking him out and giving him a look of approval. Although a little chunky, Braya was a very pretty girl. She had feather curls that sat two inches off her head, with tapered sides and back. Waleek didn't hesitate to go for her. He wasn't surprised when she bit the bait. She wasn't who he really wanted; however, Waleek figured he'd do what he had to do to stay as close as he could to what he was really after.

⚜

"SHIT BOOMING, I SEE," Mitch smiled at Pop as he looked around at the unusual surge of traffic in the area. He extended his hand out and dapped up his partner.

"Yeah. Nigga came through. They said that shit *right*," Pop boasted, referring to the cocaine they had been distributing to the streets.

Pop stood in front of the corner store on a bustling block in South West Philly and watched as smokers came and went like clockwork. He didn't usually hug the block. He was typically in and out; coming and going to distribute work to his team. Since they were moving things so fast and stayed close by in the area.

"Yeah that's wassup. We just need to figure out a way to get that shit in a much larger quantity." Mitch leaned up against Asia's truck while he spoke. He was still using her vehicle to get around. He still didn't feel comfortable enough to drop a large sum of cash on his own.

"Well, you know that's about it from boy," Pop said solemnly. "He don't move on that level. Any word on ya man from Delaware?"

"Yeah." Mitch rubbed his beard slowly. "Same shit. Ain't nothing poppin."

"Damn. Why can't he just turn you over to who he fuck with?" Pop asked.

"On some real shit; I never asked. But at the scale he was moving ... Whoever blessing him with the work ... ain't local."

"I feel you. Well, look. You let me know. My team is ready."

"Bet," was the only response Mitch could give.

The two men said they're goodbyes and went their separate ways. Pop heading back to roam the streets of South West, and Mitch heading back to the home he shared with Asia. For the first time in a long time, Mitch couldn't help but feel frustrated. Nothing was going how he had planned or envisioned while he was locked away. He couldn't get the dope he needed, and his funds were tight. He wasn't broke, but he wasn't getting it like he used to. It also didn't help that Asia wasn't kicking out any ass. He'd been home a while and they hadn't had sex one time. Initially, he did his best to respect her wishes with hopes that would change as time went on. Weeks later and several advances towards her, and she wasn't budging.

He didn't understand what the fuck she was holding on to. As much as Asia loved sex, he didn't understand. Everything else was normal. She was supportive and encouraging; although, not nearly as affectionate as she was in the past. Something told him that whoever she was fucking with before he came home, was either still a factor, or still on her mind. Whatever the case was, he was going to have to get his needs met elsewhere. He was a man. If she thought he was going to keep sitting around without sex; she was delusional. He loved Asia, but something had to give.

❧ 17 ❧

"So, this what we doing now!" Muff screamed.

Waleek was standing in the shower with soap suds on his body when Muff snatched the liner and curtain back and proceeded to jam the phone in his face. Ignoring his nakedness, she stood angrily and waited for a reply. The nigga had some explaining to do, or this was only the beginning of her tirade.

"What the fuck are you talking about?"

Waleek hadn't even been in the shower for five minutes and she was already going through his shit. His phone was in his pants pockets in the bathroom with him. Far away from her ass. She must have snuck in and grabbed them. It was always some bullshit with her.

"Nigga! These messages! These pictures! This the bitch from the daycare!"

She brought the phone back down to her face and scrolled through the messages between himself and Braya. They'd only been talking over the phone a few days and he'd just gotten her comfortable enough to send over some provocative pictures. Muff quickly scanned the contents of the messages and observed each picture. Some of them were pictures of Braya bent over with her ass cheeks hanging out; others were pictures of her bare

91

breast and exposed pussy. The last ones he hadn't even got the chance to look at and the sight of them almost made his dick jump. He couldn't wait to crack her ass.

"Put my phone back and stop going through my shit!" Waleek demanded as he waved the phone out of his face and turned his attention back to Asia.

He quickly rinsed off and hopped out the shower.

"Give me my shit."

He reached out for her to hand him the phone, but Muff threw it to the floor. She wasn't handing him shit; he could go fetch it, like the dog he was. Besides, she'd seen enough, and she was done being calm and courteous.

"Fuck you nigga. I let ya bum ass stay here and this is what you do."

She said it as if she were truly looking out for him and that she wasn't actually living with someone also.

"Bitch, you ain't doing me no motherfuckin' favors. I can stay with my aunt.

Waleek ignored the fact that he had just been caught up with pictures of another female in his phone. Although he and Muff weren't together, they were still fucking, and he was living there with her. It was purely out of convenience for Waleek. However, it wasn't worth it. He wasn't about to keep putting up with her going through his things, running her mouth, and making his life hell.

"Yeah, well carry ya broke ass over there then! You got me fucked up. You think you gon' be fuckin' this and that bitch while I sit up in this house and don't do shit?" she asked.

Waleek glared at her while he ran a dry towel over his body and quickly dried off. He immediately began shoving on his clothes so he could get the fuck away from her.

"Bet," was all he said in response. He didn't have time to argue with her drama-filled ass. There were a dozen other hoes he could stick dick in that wouldn't give him half the headache.

He scooped his phone from out the corner of the bathroom

floor where it had landed after Muff had thrown it. He quickly shoved it into his pocket. When he went to walk out, Muff blocked his path.

"Where you going?" she asked angrily. She was mad but she really didn't want him to go.

"Yo ... get the fuck out my way," he said coolly. He did his best not to match her energy. She simply wasn't worth it.

He pushed past her and headed down the hall towards her room to grab his hat. He wished he had a car. He had only been home for a week and hadn't made enough moves to have one yet.

"I swear to God, you better start telling me what the fuck is going on with you and that bitch from the daycare!" she demanded.

Waleek looked at Muff like she'd lost her mind. One minute she was telling him to get out and the next minute she wanted answers. She wasn't doing shit but stalling for time. She didn't really want to argue. She wanted him to beg her not to leave. He wasn't going to; because frankly, he didn't give a fuck about how she felt. To be honest; he no longer gave a fuck about Muff either. All the love he had for her flew out the door the day she gave his name up to them people. Staying with her was convenient for now because it was right in the same hood that he hustled in. He chose to stay there. He didn't have to. He could stay at his auntie house in North Philly. Besides, he was no dummy. He knew that Muff didn't give a fuck about anyone but herself. She only wanted him there so she could continue fucking him and stay in his pockets. He couldn't deny that she did both of those things very well. She could call him broke all she wanted; he didn't give a fuck because he didn't intend to stay broke.

"Whatever yo. I'm not about to argue with you. You told me to get out, so I'm gone."

He grabbed his hat and left while Muff stood in the middle of the room looking like a damn fool. She was furious, and the only way she knew how to deal with her anger ... was by releasing it.

⚜

"Oh shit!" Keke gasped and covered her mouth. The sound of shattering glass had drawn her to the front of the daycare where she worked. After running to the noise, she stood in shock as she watched a petite, brown-skinned girl running away from the front entrance. Keke had only caught a glimpse of her face, but she immediately recognized her.

"Brayaaaaa!" she yelled for her to come out; although it wasn't necessary since everyone had heard the impact and were now walking over.

Broken glass lay all over the floor in the front lobby of the center. The staff crowded around the front to survey the damage. When Braya finally emerged from the back, she couldn't do anything but stand there in astonishment. She couldn't believe someone had literally hurled a brick through the lobby window.

"Fuck," she mumbled quietly as she came out of her daze. "Zoe grab me my phone out Asia's office. It's on the desk by the computer," she said to one of the teacher's assistants.

She needed to call Asia and let her know what had happened before she called the police. Asia was going to be pissed. She had only run out to get coffee. She would be returning to chaos.

"Did anyone see who did the shit?" she needlessly asked.

She already knew who it was, but she was going to play it off, or else Asia was going to be big mad. Waleek had already called her and gave her the heads up. Muff had seen their messages. She should have known from Asia's rundown of her character, that she would soon be on a rampage. She actually thought she had been exaggerating. Now she knew first-hand how Maniac Muff got down.

"Yeah, I saw who did it." Keke spun around and looked at her. "It was Kayla's mom."

"Ok. You know you're going to have to make a statement to the police when they get here. I'm going to call Asia and then pull Kayla's old file to get their address."

Just as Zoe was returning with her phone, Asia was also returning. She had a bewildered look on her face and her mouth hung open as she stepped through the door of her business.

"What the fuck happened?" she asked, looking around to survey the damage.

She closed the door behind her and stopped. There was glass everywhere.

"Kayla's mom threw a brick through the window?" Braya replied.

"Fuckin' bitch," she mumbled. "You saw her do it?" she asked.

She tiptoed around the glass, being careful not to step on any. She didn't want to accidentally track any pieces back into the center where the children were. As she sat the tray of Dunkin Donut's coffee down on the counter, Keke replied.

"Yeah. I did."

"Okay. Well ... look. Everybody get back. I don't want anyone out here because I don't want to track any of this glass back in. At the end of the day, when the parents come in, advise them to enter through the back. As a matter of fact ... Braya make a note and I'll put it on the door."

While Braya scurried off to make the note, Asia grabbed her phone out of her bag and began taking pictures. As much as she hated to call the law; she knew she had no choice. It was the only way that her insurance would cover it. She didn't understand what the fuck Muff's problem was. *Why dis bitch fuckin' with me all ready?* she thought. She didn't want Waleek's ass, and she had made that very clear to him. This type of behavior wasn't like Muff though ... to antagonize her this way. It was usually phone calls and text messages. Perhaps, it was because she nor Waleek had her number. Things just didn't add up. Muff would fight, harass, and antagonize, but this was some new shit she was on. Whatever the case was; Asia knew she was going to have to get to the bottom of it and put a stop to it. She didn't have time for the nut shit, and she wasn't about to let anyone play with her money *or* her business.

After taking pictures, Asia called the police to file a police report. After they came and took pictures, she called her insurance company, and then finally called Mitch. To her surprise, he didn't argue. To him, something wasn't adding up.

"Where the nigga be at?" Mitch asked, after Asia ran down the story of what happened. He asked about Waleek's whereabouts as if he was the one who had actually thrown the brick.

"What?" Asia replied in disbelief. *Is this nigga listening to me?* she thought.

"Where does he be? I'm gonna holla at him."

"Holla at him about what Mitch?" Asia asked, growing irritated.

She didn't understand why he wanted to talk to Waleek. That wasn't going to do anything but make the situation worse.

"So, I can find out what the fuck is going on. I want to know why sis won't leave you alone. If you no longer fuckin' him ... what's the problem?"

"Mitch ... whatever. I don't even know why I told you," she mumbled.

She hadn't said anything to him but the past week he had been acting weird. She knew that things weren't going the way he wanted and that he was stressed, but lately he had been moody and a little distant. He had been coming in later and was also hanging more with Pop in South West Philly.

"You don't have to tell me. I'll find out either way."

"Mitch, you don't gotta find out shit because it isn't necessary!"

Asia glanced around and noticed her voice was traveling. A few of her staff members were looking over at her and pretending not to eavesdrop. She told Mitch to hold on and she excused herself while she walked out to sit in her truck and talk.

"You going to Waleek about this, isn't going to do anything but make shit worse. Forget I even told you. I'll handle it."

There was no way in hell she was letting Mitch approach Waleek.

"Yeah. Handle it. If not, I will. Don't forget ... my son was in there each time that bitch came up there with the bullshit. That makes it my business ... to let that fuck nigga know he needs to check his girl and figure out why the fuck she drawlin over a broad he no longer fuckin'. *So you say*," he added.

Asia didn't even bother to respond. She simply hung up her phone and silenced it. She didn't know what the fuck Mitch's problem was, but she didn't have time for it.

❦

"HELLO? HELLO?" Mitch looked down at his phone and realized Asia had hung up on him. He shoved his phone back in his pocket and jumped up from the kitchen table, where he was seated. He hated to argue with Asia, but he was frustrated. He still couldn't find a connect that could supply him on the level he needed. He wasn't making nearly as much money as he could; nor moving nearly as many drugs as he could either. After breaking off his crew, helping Asia with her expenses, and giving the lawyer money; there wasn't much left. He felt like less of a man. To top it off; Asia didn't want to fuck him. He'd touched her the other night and she brushed him off. A part of him felt like she was only with him out of sympathy, or some sort of feeling of obligation. His insecurities were starting to show, and he couldn't help but lash out. This was not how he thought his return home would be.

Mitch grabbed his jacket and walked out of the condo. It was still early in the day and he didn't want to be in the house. Since Asia had the truck, Pop was going to pick him up so they could hang out. When he finally arrived, Mitch wasted no time venting about everything that was going on.

"Sounds like you need a drink," Pop suggested after listening to his man spill his guts about his girl.

"Hell yeah. You got something in here?" Mitch asked. Pop was notorious for always keeping a bottle of Hennessey tucked somewhere in the car.

"You already," he said with a grin. "Reach in there and grab it."

Mitch grabbed the bottle out of the glove compartment, popped the top and threw the bitter liquid back. He continued to sip quietly as Pop drove.

"So you think she still fuckin' with the yo from Germantown?" Pop asked.

Somewhere in route, the liquor had kicked in and Mitch was spilling his guts to his long-term friend.

"I don't even know what to think for real. She gave me this bullshit excuse to why she won't fuck wit' me. The condo she in is paid for ... Paid for, my nigga," he said with a bewildered look. "Like ... Somebody dropped over a hundred grand for that jawn." He shook his head as if he still couldn't believe it.

"She claimed she had a beamer but when I get home, she has a fuckin' Benz that's paid for. Two fucking daycares," he vented. "I mean ... I'm proud of her ... but she secretive as shit. I was helping her when I was in the joint, but the numbers still don't add up. Where the fuck she get all that bread from?"

He shook his head and stared out the window in thought.

"I don't' know what to tell you on that my nigga," Pop said. "I don't see Asia on no creeping shit. She don't strike me as the type. Never heard her name surfacing in the streets on no hoe shit," he added. All he was trying to do was reassure Mitch there was nothing to worry about. He could tell that it was starting to fuck with his head. He needed him to be focused so he could get to the bag.

"You already know what I told you nigga. She ain't trying to kick out ... find you a quiet little jawn ... or shitttt, even a little freak bitch to get you right. Pussy is everywhere."

"You right about that," Mitch agreed with a chuckle.

He'd been home over a month. It was time for him to get some ass. He was going to fall back on pressing her for sex. He loved her, and he also knew that shit was now new to her too. He was going to focus on the money and let shit play out.

"Ay, I forgot to remind you that my son's birthday this weekend. We gon' have him a little birthday party Saturday. Bring your kids. Oh! And I invited the plug ... Well, my old plug. He flying out. He got nieces and figured it would be a nice little trip for them."

"Bet," Pop agreed. He'd definitely be there.

❧ 18 ❧

It was October 30th, and Hasan's Elmo themed birthday party was being held at Asia's Mt. Airy daycare. That particular site was larger, and it was also in a better area. Asia didn't want anything, *or anyone*; namely Muff to mess up her son's day. Although it was the end of October and still chilly; it was still warm enough for the kids to enjoy the Elmo bounce house that Asia had rented. Because the space wasn't too big, she'd gotten a smaller one, and had only invited a handful of children.

Asia had left out briefly and was now returning with the cupcakes and ice cream she'd ordered from Shoprite. As she walked in, she couldn't help but smile at all the children running around and having fun. As much as she liked order; there was none. The kids were literally running all over, laughing, and having a ball. Red, helium-filled balloons adorned the ceilings; there was face painting, and Asia had even hired an entertainer dressed as Elmo, to walk around, play with, and take pictures with the kids. Hasan loved Elmo, and Mitch and Asia spared no expense to make sure that he was well represented at their son's party. She'd invited several members of her staff that also had toddlers. They were helping her, while their own children ran amok. To show her appreciation, *and like typical black folks*, she had alcoholic beverages stashed in the office for all the adults. She'd had a few drinks herself and was feeling very relaxed in the chaotic environment.

Asia went to sit down the food she was carrying. Before she could get to the designated table, she was almost knocked over by a child that had dashed through. *Where the hell was Mitch?* He was supposed to be helping her bring in the items from the car. She was thankful she hadn't dropped anything.

"Braya, can you make sure he stays in the back where the bounce house is," Asia said. The little person in question was a toddler named Richard. He was notoriously hyper and had been running through the center from the time the party started.

"Girl ... I tried," Braya replied from her where she was seated in the corner with a few other co-worker guests. Braya got up and went to grab him.

"Where's Mitch," she mumbled to no one in particular. "Mitch!" she called out. She went to call him again, but he emerged from the back.

"Right here babe," he said. "Look who dropped in."

He smiled as he approached her. Josiah walked in behind him. A pretty, older woman that appeared to be his mother also came behind him, while another woman that looked a little older than herself trailed closely as well. She knew right away that the second woman was his sister. Her and Josiah looked strikingly similar. She had shoulder-length, brown curly hair and her skin was an exquisite shade of golden brown. Asia was almost at a loss for words. Meeting his family had come as a surprise.

"Wassup Asia," Josiah said.

"Uhh ... Hi," she stammered.

Mitch noticed her tense up when she saw Josiah and his family. He shot her a puzzled look. She was acting weird. His face quickly softened when he noticed her relax a little. *Probably the liquor*, he thought to himself. She would smoke a little, but Asia wasn't much of a drinker.

"Hey Josiah. I'm sorry. I didn't expect to see you here," she waved.

Asia let out a nervous giggle. "I had a few drinks," she admitted. "Hi, how are you," she said, greeting Lolita, and Maria. "You must be Josiah's mom ..." Asia paused and waited for her to tell her.

"Lolita," she said with a warm smile.

"And you must be his ..."

"Sister," Maria smiled. "Maria."

"Nice to meet you both. You can help yourself to anything we have here. We have cake, ice cream, and pizza for the kids. I would have gotten something fancier if I knew we were going to have special guests."

"No, you're just fine honey. We are in the area all day so I promise we're going to eat up as much as we can. Maria has twin girls; so pizza, cake and ice cream is just fine, thank you. We'll be in the back with them. It was nice meeting you,"

The two women smiled politely and disappeared back into the outside where the bounce house was set up and blocking the alleyway. Before Asia could utter another word, Mitch began speaking.

"Babe listen. We bout to go chop it up for a bit out front. I want to introduce Josiah to Pop. Let me know if you need me for anything, and if I'm not back when you ready to sing Happy Birthday, come get me."

"Okay," she said.

While Mitch was speaking she had to force herself to keep from taking glances at Josiah, who was standing behind him. She hated when Mitch put her in awkward situations. She also hated that Mitch was ditching his responsibilities of helping her with their son's birthday party, but she wasn't going to even make a fuss about it. Seeing Josiah had her thrown off and had completely altered her mood; although she was going to do her best to play it off. She watched him walk off behind Mitch. He looked so good, and when he was standing near her; she could smell the sweet but masculine scent of his cologne wafting off of him. *Why the fuck would Mitch invite this nigga?* she thought to herself angrily. For weeks she'd done nothing but push thoughts of Josiah from her mind and now she was being forced to face him. Every feeling that she had damn near killed herself to suppress, had come back full force. The liquor she had been drinking didn't make it any better. She wanted to talk to him, but she knew she couldn't.

Fuck it, she thought. She reached to her side and dug her phone out of her purse. She prayed he still had the same number. She had erased it out of her contacts but still had the ten digits logged into her memory. After she punched them in, she typed, *Meet me at Mama Bella's at nine. We need to talk.* His mother said they were going to be in the city for the remainder of the day, so she knew he wouldn't be far. The Josiah that she knew would drive from Wilmington to Philly at the last minute to see her. While she nervously waited for a response, she continued to play the host of her son's birthday party. A few minutes later, she heard her phone vibrate and ding from inside her purse. It was Josiah. She swiped her phone open to read his response.

Ok, was his reply. A wave of relief rushed over her. A new set of jitters now overcame her. She was meeting Josiah later for them to talk. *What the fuck did I just do?* were now her new thoughts.

❧ 19 ❧

At the end of Hasan's birthday party, Josiah loaded both the twins into the back of the rented, black Suburban and slammed the door. Both the girls were slumped over and sleeping after the days' festivities. He had no doubt they were worn out after all the running around they did. Josiah's mother and sister had already hopped inside of the truck and were already in seat-belts when he slid into the driver's seat and began digging in his pocket for the key.

"Is that *her*?" his mother randomly asked from the passenger seat beside him.

"Huh?" he asked, shooting her a look as if he had no idea what and who she was talking about.

He stopped fumbling for the key and looked at her for a moment. Her expression was grim, but it instantly softened when she looked at his face and in his eyes. Lolita knew her boy, and she had no doubt that he loved the woman that she had just met. Josiah looked into the rearview mirror and glared at his sister. He could tell Maria knew what was up as soon she was introduced to Asia. He was sure Trish had told her everything she'd overheard. Maria always had a big mouth. He had no doubt that his sister had certainly made their mother aware as well of the "real" reason behind their most recent argument.

"Yeah, that was her," he said solemnly while staring at the road listlessly.

Finally locating his keys, he pushed them into the ignition, started the truck and pulled out of the parking space.

"Okay," she nodded. "Well, do you wanna tell me why the hell you're playing with fire?" she asked while she adjusted the strap of her seatbelt and made herself comfortable for the ride back to Josiah's house in Wilmington.

Josiah didn't respond right away. He instead, continued to stare straight ahead in hopes that she would eventually let up.

"Answer me Josiah. Why are you playing with fire? Why the hell would you attend their child's birthday party knowing that you were sleeping with her?" she demanded to know. No matter how lovestruck he was, it was a foolish move.

"Because he asked me to ... okay," Josiah replied firmly. "It's his son's second birthday and he asked me to come. I figured we all could use a little getaway, so I agreed.

Lolita eyed her son. She could tell when he was lying or telling half-truths. She continued to stare at him, so he knew that she knew, he was full of shit. Josiah glanced ahead nervously. Finally, he sighed and then proceeded to explain.

"Look ... Mitch introduced us. You already know how he and I met ... In the city jail and we became fast friends. You also already know he ended up with a crazy prison sentence, but despite all that; we were still working together. I had some strings pulled on the outside, so that he could make moves on the inside. Initially, I had to go through her to get the money. One thing led to another and the next thing you know ... we were together. Or so I thought. I mean ... you saw her in there. She's beautiful, charming and honest. I couldn't help but fall for her ... The whole time he was fighting for an appeal. She didn't know he would get it, and neither did I. We supported him, but with the numbers he'd gotten; no one ever expected for him to come home. I wanted to tell him months ago, but she wasn't ready yet. He would've been mad, but he would have accepted it. But, she wouldn't do it. She was scared. Then, boom. He wins an appeal and gets another shot at freedom. Just like that, we were finished."

"Well it doesn't look finished to me," his mother added dryly. "As silly and shocked as she looked, it doesn't look like she's over you as well."

"So, he doesn't know?" Maria asked, butting in from the backseat.

Josiah smacked his teeth. "Of course he doesn't. I told you; she was too scared to tell him. Which forced me to fall back."

"So, you love her?" Lolita asked, although she didn't have to. She could see it in his eyes. She could see it in how he looked at her; how he interacted with her.

"Yeah," he replied without hesitating. "Can we change the subject though please," he asked.

Without replying, both Lolita and Maria agreed. Lolita however, was worried. She had noticed that Asia seemed to be much like Josiah: in love. Although they tried to play it off; she didn't miss it. *Hell* ... she wondered; if she'd noticed it, did Josiah's friend Mitch notice as well. As much as she loved her son, she always knew that woman would be his downfall.

🌿 20 🌿

"Hey babe, you want me to start taking that bounce house down?" Mitch asked, approaching Asia from behind while she used a clear spray bottle and paper towels to spray down the counter, table, and anything left nasty and sticky from the kids. Everyone had left and they were now cleaning up and preparing to leave.

"No, you're good. The company I rented it from is going to take it down and carry it out tomorrow. "

"Cool. Look babe, I know you're tired. You got it clean enough in here. Why don't you go home and get some rest," he urged.

He was hoping she was almost done. Secretly, he was ready to go. He wanted to meet Pop and handle some business. He looked around and the place looked restored to its original condition. He didn't understand what she was still cleaning.

"Rest." Asia glanced at the clock on the wall. "It's only six o clock."

The party had started at noon, and although it had been a long day; it was still early.

"Yeah. I just figured you were tired after such a long day."

"I'm good. I do this on the regular. You got plans or something?" Asia asked curiously as she continued to shuffle around the center while Mitch followed her.

She began putting back her cleaning supplies, throwing away her used paper towels, and turning off lights.

"Not really. I'll probably chill with Pop a little bit down Southwest. See how things moving along down there."

At first Asia wasn't going to protest. She wanted to slide out for a little bit to take care of some business anyway. Although ... she wasn't fond of the fact that Mitch had been hanging out so much in the hood with Pop. He'd been acting a little strange lately and she was sure it had something to do with him being around old friends and old habits.

"Why you keep hanging down there so much? You not touching nothing," she reminded him, referring to the drugs he slung. "So, why you gotta babysit every day?" she asked.

She grabbed her purse and jacket in preparation to leave. However, she stopped and stood in the middle of the dark room and waited for Mitch's response.

"'Cuz it ain't shit else to do and I get tired of sitting in the fuckin' house. It's Saturday. Hasan is gone and it ain't like shit else poppin," he said sarcastically.

Asia glared at him and threw her hand to her hip. His sarcastic remark hadn't flown over her head and she could detect a whole lot of discontent. She wanted to know what the fuck his problem was.

"The fuck that mean?"

"It means what I said. Ain't shit else poppin. Look, can we go?" he asked impatiently.

He didn't wait for a response. He headed toward the door to leave. Asia trailed behind him.

"Clarify that. What you mean, *ain't shit else poppin?*"

"You know what it mean. You not fuckin'," he snapped. "You in and out for work, and I'm not doing shit but sitting in the crib. That shit boring. I hustle, so, when the sun sets and I can go check on my money and my people; it shouldn't be a problem. And ... You in and out mentally. What the fuck is up with you?" he blurted.

She was getting on his damn nerves and he figured if she wanted to pick an argument; he might as well lay all that shit on the line at one time.

"Nothing's up with me," she grumbled.

She pushed past Mitch to walk out the door, but before she could grab the handle, he grabbed her arm and turned her back around to face him.

"Yes it is, and we bout to clear the air right now. Since, you want to put shit out in the open and ask me questions. I think it's about time I start asking you some. What's up with you? You distant, *and* I've been home for how long now? And you won't fuck me ... So, the question is ... Who you fuckin? Who got you so preoccupied that you don't fuck with me?" Mitch stared her down and waited for a response.

Fuck, Asia thought. She was the worst liar, and even if she tried to lie, Mitch would see right through her and pick that shit apart.

"Mitch ... Now's not the time," she stammered, doing her best to worm her way out of questioning.

"Now's the perfect time. You got somewhere to be?" he asked, knowing damn well she didn't.

Asia felt nervousness envelop her, while perspiration began to form on her nose.

"Talk, Asia. How about ... I be more specific. Are you back fuckin' with the nigga Waleek?"

"What?" she smacked her teeth in frustration and shook her head "no."

She couldn't believe he was forcing her to have this conversation in the middle of a dead and dark ass daycare center.

"Well, what's up with you? When I came home, you said that

you were dealing with someone. Apparently, this someone has you questioning whether you want to be with me or not. So, who is it?" he asked, his tone and demeanor, all of a sudden, much more serious.

The question caused a cold chill to sweep through Asia, although the person in question gave her nothing but feelings of warmth. Her expression gave her away. Mitch was genuinely curious, and she knew that he wouldn't stop until he got an answer. Asia didn't know how she was going to tell him. *Fuck*, she thought. *Should I try and lie?* she quickly asked herself.

"Who is he Asia? Tell me."

Asia parted her lips and went to speak but nothing came out but air.

"Who is he? Who's the person that's got you so mentally consumed. Is it someone from Germantown? Someone you met after Waleek? Someone you did business with?"

As soon as he mentioned, "*someone she did business with*"; she looked up at him painfully. She couldn't do it anymore. She couldn't keep carrying that weight on her shoulder. She was tired of lying and tired of hiding. It was time for her to start being honest, and there was no better time than now.

"Someone you did business with?" Mitch asked. Now he was getting somewhere.

"Okay. So who the fuck is it?"

Finally, out of nowhere, Asia got the courage to speak. "Someone I did business with ... and someone you did business with as well," she murmured.

What the hell is she getting at? he thought.

"What?" he asked. He didn't understand what the fuck she was talking about and he was tired of talking in fucking riddles. "Who Asia? Say his fuckin' name."

"Mitch ... " Asia hesitated. She wanted to tell him so bad.

"Say his name Asia."

"Josiah," she said softly. Her lip trembled as she looked into Mitch's eyes and waited for a response.

A wave of nausea overcame him. Mitch felt like he had all the wind knocked out of him.

"What?" he snapped. "Josiah? You gotta be bullshittin'," he said.

He took a step back away from Asia and stood in the middle of the lobby and just glared at her. How could she? It felt like betrayal. "Josiah, Asia?"

"It ... Just happened," she stammered. "It was never either of our intention to cross y----"

"Shut the fuck up Asia! I only did business with the nigga for three months through the joint. You mean to tell me that neither of y'all was on no snake shit? Y'all was only around each other, for three fuckin' months!" he yelled. "So, you only needed that little bit of fuckin' time to cross me!"

"Mitch ... That wasn't my intention. I swear it wasn't," she pleaded. "You had so much time, and I was going through a breakup with Waleek. Then here comes Josiah. He was there for me ... There for you. And shit just happened. I never wanted to take it there, but he thought you would respect a man like him, stepping in and looking out for us."

"Yeah ... He did that didn't he," Mitch replied sarcastically. "Shit makes sense now. The car. The deed. Everything makes sense."

There was no fuckin' way he could compete with that nigga on the money tip. Mitch paused for a minute to take everything in. He shook his head solemnly. As angry as he was, he couldn't help but understand. He had been given football numbers, and Asia's life didn't stop. As much as he wanted to believe it did, he knew that it didn't. While he continued to absorb everything, he also learned something else: who believed in him and who didn't.

As hard as he was going for his appeal, no one thought he would get it. Yeah, they'd listened, but when it all boiled down to it; no one believed that he was going to get it. Let alone, come home. No one but Pop that is. Out of all the people in his corner, he was proving to be the realest. It was crazy that his homeboy believed in him more than his woman. While still in thought, Asia looked at Mitch and didn't know what to say. He had every right to be upset. He was actually taking it a lot better than what she thought he would.

"So, Josiah bought you the crib?" he asked for clarity. He had to know.

"Yeah," she said solemnly.

Asia truly felt bad. She felt bad that she hurt Mitch, but she didn't feel bad for how she felt about Josiah. She loved him, and as desperately as she tried to shake and suppress the feelings; she couldn't.

"So, tell me this Asia." Mitch paused for a moment. "What do you want to do? Because clearly ... whatever relationship you had with him has you feeling confused or some shit," he accused.

Asia didn't know how to answer that. In a perfect world, she would sail off into the sunset with Josiah by her side ... But also in that perfect world, Mitch was absent from it. Deep down, she wanted her cake, and she wanted to eat it too. However, she knew she couldn't do it. With Mitch back home, it was hard for her to decide. She loved Mitch. He was all she knew before he went to prison. Josiah however, taught her that life could also be beautiful with another man. Having Mitch around complicated things though. Being with the father of her child is where she felt like she was *supposed* to be.

"I'm with you," she said softly, looking up at him. "I just need time to adjust to everything."

"Need time to adjust? How fuckin' long is that Asia?" Mitch asked angrily.

He was mad, but he wasn't even going to act like he wasn't part of the problem. He had sent a rich nigga into his girl's life. *His beautiful girl*, at that. He'd put her on a pedestal, and she didn't belong there. Asia was human, and she had made a mistake. Josiah wasn't a fucked-up nigga, so he didn't have a whole lot to say other than what she did was wrong. However, the more and more he thought to himself, the more he realized, he'd created a recipe for disaster. As much as Mitch wanted to strangle Asia and Josiah, he had to be an adult about the entire situation.

He waited for Asia to reply. When she failed to do so, Mitch went back to talking.

"Look ... I'm a man. I know I left you fucked up," he sighed before continuing. "That fucks with me every day. That's exactly why I did what I did and grind how I grind; to make sure that'll never be the case again. I could be a bitter nigga and go off on you; but at the end of the day, you don't deserve that. My hands caused this. You know that I'd do anything for you ... and you know that I love you. You know I'll take care of you. But ... I know that he will too. He showed that," Mitch said, forcing the words out.

He couldn't believe he was going to say the shit he was about to say. He didn't want to, but it was the right thing. He felt like a cold bitch, but he loved Asia, and he wanted nothing more than for her and his son to be happy and cared for.

"Whatever choice you want to make Asia ... make it. I know you love me. And I'm starting to think that you love that nigga too. You need to make a choice. I love you and I want to see you happy. But ... at the same time, I would like for you to want to see me happy too. If you fucked up behind that nigga, you not going to put that energy into working on our relationship."

Asia looked at him with tears spilling from her eyes but didn't say a word. He was right.

"I'm gon' give you the space you need, but if you not all for me, then I gotta move on. At this point, I don't even know what my future holds. Especially with these appeals looming over my head. I need to be sure that whoever I'm with, is rocking 100%. With me ... and only me," he said.

Mitch looked to the door.

"I gotta get some air. I'm gon' walk to my mom's from here." His mother didn't live very far.

"I'll get Pop to pick me up from there."

"Okay," Asia replied with a sniffle.

She watched Mitch walk out the door, and for the first time in months; it felt like a weight had been lifted off her shoulders.

❦ 21 ❦

The text that Asia had sent to Josiah earlier asked him to meet her at 9 o'clock. Asia glanced nervously at her dashboard. It was 8:50. Even though she was early; Josiah was earlier. As she approached the front of Mama Bella's, she saw that he was already there, standing on the curb waiting for her. He had changed his clothes and now wore fitted black jeans and a Ralph Lauren sweater. She could tell the brand because it had a big dumb-ass, brown bear on the front of it. She killed the engine to her truck, and then she reached up and pulled down her visor so she could check her make up. She already knew her outfit was cute. Before she met Josiah, she'd stopped home and showered. When she got dressed, she didn't want to overdo it and looked like she was trying too hard. For that reason, she chose a sleeveless, black, midi-dress. She threw a long sweater over it to be modest. With her gold jewelry to accessorize, she still looked simple and beautiful

Although she had seen Josiah's earlier, she was still nervous and wanted to make sure she looked presentable. After verifying that her hair was still bone-straight and intact, she slathered on a final coat of gloss. *Here goes nothing*, she thought, before hopping out of the car. After arguing with Mitch and freeing her conscious; she felt like a heavy weight had been lifted off her shoulders. However, her emotions were all over the place. She just wanted to talk to Josiah; see where his head was and how he was doing. As she approached, she greeted him with a warm smile; however, the friendly gesture wasn't reciprocated. *I see he isn't going to make this easy*, she thought to herself. Although his face was expressionless, when she stared into Josiah's eyes, she could see the hurt. Asia understood why he was so distant and angry. He had every right to be. Josiah wasn't into playing games; especially over the woman that he loved.

"Hey," Asia greeted him as she walked off the street and stepped up onto the curb where he was standing.

He replied with a simple, "*wassup.*"

"Damn, no hug?" she asked, doing her best to try and break the ice.

"You could've hugged me earlier when you saw me," Josiah replied bitterly as he gave Asia the once over. He hated that she was so beautiful.

Asia sighed at Josiah's response. He wasn't going to make things easy for her.

"Okay, well do you want to go inside and get something to eat instead of standing out here looking like you ready to rob the place," she asked, trying to ease the tension between them with a little humor.

"I'm not really hungry," he said quickly before peering at her.

Asia knew by his pending look that he was about to go left.

"What I'm trying to figure out, is what you called me here for? Why do we need to meet and what do we need to talk about?" he asked.

Asia couldn't help but notice the urgency and growing impatience in his voice. She knew Josiah was going to be difficult, but she had no idea that he was going to act this cold towards her.

"Josiah, why you acting so cold? I missed you, and I just wanted to talk to you about everything that's been going on. How's life? How you been?"

"Shouldn't you be talking to Mitch?" he countered. "I mean ... Y'all doing the family thing and all. Birthday parties ... Him calling you babe. I wonder what else he calls you," he said jealously.

"What's that supposed to mean?" Asia asked, defensively. "I haven't slept with him if that's what you're insinuating."

"Yeah, sure," he scoffed.

"This is hard for me too, Josiah. I love you, but I also love him," she trembled, becoming emotional. "You think I wanted things to be like this. I'm glad that Mitch is home, but I hate that we can't be together," she admitted, fluid lining the rim of her eyes.

Asia hated that she felt the way she did. She just wanted to be happy. She hated that Josiah was treating her the way he was. Seeing her break down and become emotional softened Josiah's cold disposition.

"Don't cry Asia," he said softly.

He reached out and wiped her tear. When he did, she grabbed his arm and held it to her face. It had been so long. She just wanted to touch him again. For him to hold her. Being so close to Asia brought back all the feelings he felt when he was with her. It had been a long time since he'd touched her. Without thinking, Josiah leaned down and pressed his lips into Asia's. Like butter, they melted into one another's. Just as she remembered, Josiah's lips were pillowy soft and warm. It had been a while since she had been touched intimately. And although Mitch was there, ready and willing. Her body yearned for Josiah.

Judging by the heat and passion of his kiss; she could tell that he longed for her just as much. Just as she let out a low groan, she pulled away. She should have known this was a bad idea. She wanted Josiah so bad, her body literally ached for him. Seeing her hesitate, caused Josiah to grow angry. He stood there for a second and peered down at her sadly. *Damn*, he thought. *If only you would just choose me.*

No matter how much she professed her love for him, he knew that they still would never be. Asia looked down and folded her arms across her body. She was at a loss for words and was embarrassed. Josiah waited for her to say something, but when she didn't, he decided to do all the talking.

"I told you I can't do this Asia. You know I love you, but I can't cross Mitch like that. Before ... the circumstances were different. He was locked up and you were my girl." He paused. "Well, I thought you were my girl. But now is different. You're his girl. You gotta stay the fuck over there. You can't keep playing both sides. You chose Mitch."

"You didn't give me a chance to choose," she stammered.

"You not choosing was a choice. ... You chose him. It's been months," he said. "I can't play this game with you. I won't share the woman that I love. I won't share," he added for finality." As much as I love you Asia, you need to lose my number and don't hit me up again. Any business with Mitch, is just that. Business with Mitch."

He looked at her and Asia could see the pain in his eyes. She knew he didn't want to do what he was doing, but he had to. She understood it, but she didn't like it. Josiah was forcing himself to shut her out. Forcing himself to be so cold.

Josiah began backing away from her hesitantly.

"I gotta go Asia. I'll see you around," he said before leaving her and heading down the street towards where his SUV was parked.

Asia stood there dumbfounded and blinked back hot tears. As she watched him fade into the distance it felt like a part of her heart was fading with him. As much as she didn't want it to be she knew it was over. Feeling pathetic and rejected, Asia headed home. She was going to push Josiah to the back of her mind. The only way she knew how to do that was by becoming busy. She was going to immerse herself into her work and focus on her and Mitch's relationship.

The only way he was going to win his appeal was by keeping

his lawyer paid and having faith. She decided that she wasn't going to let him fight his legal battle alone. Despite what her heart screamed for her to do; she was going to do the opposite. She was going to move forward with Mitch. Even if they didn't work out, she wasn't going to reach out to Josiah again.

❧ 22 ❧

"I brought donuts!" Asia yelled a few days later, as she walked through the door of her Mt. Airy daycare.

Although she spent most of her time at her Germantown location; she often went back and forth between them throughout the week, to make sure things were running smoothly.

As Asia approached the counter and sat down the box containing the dozen donuts she'd purchased, she noticed a middle-aged, Caucasian gentleman walking through and observing her daycare. He had a clipboard in his hand and looked like he was there for business purposes. She noticed no one was with him. Usually, Braya was on top of everything; however, she had called out sick the past couple of days. While everyone was nestled in their classroom, no one seemed to be paying their visitor no attention. Asia frowned. *Who the fuck is he?* she thought. She'd never seen him before.

"Hi, Sir. I'm Asia, the owner. Who might you be?" she asked, approaching him and extending her hand to introduce herself.

"I'm Clark Berry."

He flashed a beaming white smile and shook Asia's hand. Although older, he was a handsome white man. Well-dressed and clean-cut with silver hair that was neatly combed against his head.

"I'm from the PA Department of Human Services, Child Care Licensing Department."

Asia was confused. Both her daycare's had been inspected and held all necessary licenses to operate.

"I'm sorry," she smiled, still unsure of why he was standing in her place of business. "I'm confused, Mr. --- uhhhhh.,"

She did her best to recall his name.

"Clark. You can call me Clark. Is there uhhh, somewhere we can go and talk?" he asked, noticing her staff's piercing eyes as they eavesdropped from their small classes.

"Yeah, sure. Follow me," Asia said, leading the way into her office around the corner. When they both got inside, she closed the door behind them so they could speak freely and privately.

"You can have a seat," she said, motioning for him to sit.

Asia took a spot behind her desk, while Mr. Berry sat across from her.

"So, as I mentioned before, I'm with Pennsylvania's Department of Human Services, Child Care Licensing Unit. I'm basically here because we were notified that your daycares are not compliant."

"What do you mean, *not compliant?*" Asia asked, growing uncomfortable. She wanted to know where the hell he was headed with this.

"Basically, your staff isn't certified. You're the owner of ..." He paused and looked down at his clipboard. After flipping through a few pages, he continued. "Two centers, correct? As the owner, I'm assuming you are also acting, or serving as the Director?"

"Actually, Lisa Johnson serves as Director. I'm familiar with the regulations Clark," Asia said matter-of-factly.

When Asia was in the beginning steps of opening her business, she hit a roadblock when she learned that she needed a degree in order to operate legally. Mitch advised her to hire someone who had one and allow them to oversee it remotely. As long as her paperwork was good; she was good.

"I see that your application states that; however, Lisa Johnson also serves as Director of her own two facilities in Center City. Although she has the education to serve as Director, she has to be present at each facility a minimum of 30 hours a week. Now, in order for her to do that, she'd have to work over 120 hours a week. You see where I'm going with this ..." he asked, eyeing Asia.

"What qualifications do you have?" he asked.

Asia didn't respond. She had gone from sure of herself, to worried in a matter of seconds.

"You don't have to answer that. I also see on your application that you have a year of experience at a childcare facility. Experience that you also obtained from underneath Lisa Johnson." Clark cleared his throat and eyed Asia somberly. He hated that he was going to have to do what he was about to do. "With just a year of experience, you don't qualify as Director or Supervisor of any facility in Pennsylvania. Unless you can show me that another person in here does ... I'm going to have to shut you down ... today."

Asia felt her heart drop to her feet. Everything he was saying was true, so she didn't know how to respond. She was at a loss for words. Law was law, and she knew there was no immediate solution to what she was now faced with. She did, however, have a question that she was dying to ask.

"You said earlier that you were notified that my daycares weren't compliant. Can you tell me who notified you?"

Clark got up from the chair he was sitting and prepared to leave. "I'm afraid I can't name the person. It was anonymous. I do have to advise that anytime we get a complaint or a tip from anyone, that we have to take it very seriously and look into it."

Asia didn't even bother to respond to what he said. She already knew who it was. As soon as he said, *complaint or tip*, she knew what it was. It was no one but Muff who had called. She was so mad that she was at a loss for words anyway.

"The first step is asking you to voluntarily close your doors until you are compliant. If that doesn't occur, we have to forcefully shut you down, and that entails us putting chains on the door," he added.

"That's not necessary," she grumbled. "I'll notify parents today and we will be closed at the end of the business day."

"Thank you. It was nice meeting you despite the circumstances," Mr. Berry stated before he headed out the door.

"Fuck!" Asia yelled, slamming her fist down on her wood desk.

What the fuck am I going to do! she thought. All her income would be frozen at the end the day. Going back to school took too long. She didn't have an Associate degree; let alone a Bachelor's. She had two choices. Either she hired someone to serve as Director to her centers, or she closed her doors down.

৩৩৩

AS SOON AS state had left her daycare, Asia informed her staff she had an emergency and took off. She still had to figure out how the hell she was going to notify all the parents and staff that as of today, she was going to be closed indefinitely. She tried to keep herself as calm as possible, as she drove towards her old neighborhood where her mother still lived. She cursed as she navigated through the congested traffic in Germantown; obeying the stop signs and traffic lights as she went. She was on a manhunt. She was going to find Waleek's ass and put a stop to the bullshit with Muff --- once and for all. Even if he had to call that bitch out there so they could shoot the one; she was going to end it. She was tired of the bullshit. *This bitch is fuckin' with my money. Everything I built!* she thought. Fuck fighting! The way she felt, she was ready to ride and die behind her shit.

Asia knew there were only a handful of places Waleek would

be. He was all about his money, and since it was the middle of the day *and* the beginning of the month; she knew that he was going to be posted up at one of his trap houses. She knew he probably still had them since she doubted that anyone from Germantown would fuck with Waleek or his paper. He was notorious for going to war about his money. Even if other nigga's had tried to come in while he was gone; he had a team of little nigga's that would ride to keep it.

Asia turned on Pulaski street and drove slowly, so she could scan the busy block. It had been a year since she'd stayed with her mother, and although a lot had changed in her life; nothing had seemed to change on the block. It was still dirty as fuck with beer cans clanking and rolling down the street, being pushed by the wind. Beat-up and abandoned cars still lined the sidewalk; while drunks, hookers, smokers, and dealers still littered the street.

It didn't take long for Asia to ride past Waleek's spots and get through the entire block. Out of the dozens of people she saw littered on the street, she hadn't spotted Waleek. She turned the corner and headed to his other location. Just as she drove down the dead-end street, she spotted the last person she would ever think she'd see: Braya. She was leaning against her car smiling, while Waleek leaned against her, probably whispering "sweet nothings." They were way too comfortable and friendly for Braya to lie and say it was anything other than what it looked like.

Everything was now coming together. Shit was all starting to make sense. *This sneaky bitch*, Asia thought to herself. That's why Braya was asking all those questions about Waleek and Muff the day she put Kayla out the center. It was also why Braya tried to persuade her to keep her in the center after she told her that the two were nothing but drama. Asia had confided in her, and the stupid bitch still went behind her back and started fucking with the nigga who was the center of her troubles. *I got something for her ass*, she thought. She grabbed her door handle as she drove but paused. For a second, she contemplated pulling a Muff and hopping out on Braya so she could beat her ass half to death. Then she immediately came to her senses. Waleek wasn't her nigga.

She took a deep breath and let go of her handle. Instead of pulling up and hopping out on them, Asia slowed down and parked behind another car. With her hands shaking, she dug out her phone and quickly pulled up her Dropbox app. She thanked God that she was organized and could access her daycare records from anywhere. She went through them and pulled up the phone number she was looking for. After temporarily memorizing it, she plugged it in her text messages, typed away, and pressed send.

Finally, Asia got out of her car and walked towards where Braya and Waleek were standing. Waleek's face was expressionless, while Braya looked not only shocked, but also embarrassed.

"So, I see why Muff been buggin' out lately!" Asia yelled, as she speed walked closer to the two. Braya went to open her mouth to speak, but Asia stopped her. She took a deep breath and unballed her fist. *I wanna beat this bitch sooooo bad*, she thought.

"Bitch save it. I don't even give a fuck. I came out here to talk to Waleek, and Waleek only," Asia finally replied. She turned her back to Braya and went in on Waleek.

"So, this is what you been doing that got Muff acting like a fuckin' lunatic. Bustin' the windows out my daycare ... Calling the state on me ... Getting both my daycares closed the fuck down!" she screamed.

She snapped her neck back angrily and glared at Braya who stood there dumbfounded. She truly felt like beating the curls out her damn head. She was one of the people that had witnessed her work her ass off for her businesses, and now they were being snatched from up under her for some shit that didn't even really have shit to do with her. Either Braya didn't understand, or she simply didn't give a fuck. Asia knew first-hand that it was likely the latter. She had been dicked down by Waleek; so, if Braya had gotten a taste, she probably didn't care about shit at the point. However, that was all about to change.

"Yo, I didn't know Muff was doing none of that bullshit Asia. You know how she is."

"No, nigga! *You* know how she is! Why the fuck would you fuck with somebody from my fuckin' daycare, knowing that bitch was gon' think it was me!" she yelled.

"And I already warned yo' stupid ass that his baby mama was going be drama, but yo' thirsty ass so hype over a nigga attention," she turned around and barked at Braya. "Fuckin' with this nigga got my shit closed down!"

Braya didn't have a response for what Asia was saying. All she could do was stand there silently and look scared. Her lack of response almost caused Asia to pounce on her. *Scared ass bitch*, she thought.

"My shit got shut down! The business that I bust my ass for ..."

Asia paused for a minute and looked down the street as if she was looking for someone. Just as she turned back around to continue cursing both their trifling asses out, she heard the sound she was waiting for: Muff's squealing tires as she barreled down the street. Asia smiled. They were about to settle that shit.

"Naaa, stay yo' ass here like a woman," Asia said to Braya who was shaking like a leaf during a rainstorm. "I dare you to try and run. We 'bout to get this shit straight right now," Asia said aloud, when she saw Braya try to creep off towards the driver's side of her car.

Waleek grew instantly irritated at the sight of his baby mama's arrival. He smacked his teeth and shook his head from side-to-side since he knew she was about to cause a whole scene. Muff had screeched to a stop and threw her car in park in the middle of the street. As she hopped out, any person with sense could tell, she had come to rumble. She had her long lace-front, pulled back into a ponytail; and instead of a dress, she had on sweatpants and a black t-shirt. She had just gotten the text from

Asia a few minutes ago telling her to come out to Waleek's bando on the dead-end-block. Before Muff could start going off, Asia stopped her and spoke up. She was going to lay everything out in the open. One time, and one time only.

"Look, I called you out here because we need to settle our differences right now," Asia said through clenched teeth. As much as she wanted to smack Muff's brains out her head, she figured she'd speak her peace first. She now knew why Muff had done what she had done.

"I *do not* fuck with Waleek. This bitch here does," she pointed to Braya, whose eyes grew wide.

"What that bitch does with Waleek, don't got shit to do with me. Leave me and my daycare the fuck alone!" Asia demanded.

"Girl, I ain't worried 'bout you. I already knew they was fuckin' because I saw the hoe in his phone! I go for wherever that bitch be, until I can get to her," Muff admitted with zero remorse. She didn't care whose place it was. It could be her job or her mama's house.

"Well, she's fired. So, please leave my shit alone."

As Braya leaned against her car, she looked pleadingly to Waleek, while Muff stared her down menacingly.

"He can't save you, bitch. You knew he had a family, but you still fucked him. Didn't I text you and tell you to leave him the fuck alone?" she asked, pointing towards her with an accusatory finger.

Braya didn't respond since she knew full-well that she had gotten the text from Waleek's phone indicating that it was his baby mama. She had been warned to stay away, but she didn't.

"I don't have time for this," Braya said shakily.

She came off her car and tried to hurry to the driver side, but Muff was hot on her heels. The worst thing she could have done was turn her back on a chick like Muff ... because as soon as she did, she was on her ass. Braya didn't stand a chance against her, as Muff snatched her to the ground by her hair and proceeded to beat the shit out of her.

"Ahhhhhhhhh! Get her off me!" Braya let out a piercing scream.

Asia shook her head in disappointment at Waleek, who had walked off in amusement. Asia wasn't going to lie; she wanted to see Muff beat Braya's backstabbing ass more than anyone; hence the reason she texted her to come out there. What surprised her was that Waleek was letting it go down. He had literally walked off and started laughing with some young niggas, who appeared to be his workers. Several of them had emerged from inside the house when they heard all the commotion taking place outside. Asia figured they wanted to witness the slaughter, since that was exactly what it was: a fucking slaughter. Muff was beating Braya like a slave caught wandering off.

"Waleek, you need to break them up!" Asia yelled out as Braya begged for mercy.

He quickly motioned to a couple of the guys beside him to intervene. They ran over and tried to pull Muff from off top of Braya. She was now literally sitting on her talking shit, while she occasionally spit and drove her fist into Braya's bloody, twisted and tormented face.

"Don't act like you concerned since you the mufucka that told her to come out here," he accused.

Asia rolled her eyes in response.

"'Cuz, I'm tired of her fuckin' with me. That bitch got my daycares closed down. Maybe now she can see that I'm not the fuckin' problem."

Asia didn't bother to wait for a response. She headed back to her car with Waleek following behind her.

"Asia, hold up," Waleek called.

She spun around to face him. Her face was a mixture of anger and borderline exhaustion. She had so much on her mind; the last thing she wanted to do was give Waleek or Muff's ass any more of her time or attention.

"What?" she snapped.

"So, that means, you done --- done?" he asked. "It's a rap for us? Completely over?"

Asia rolled her eyes and scoffed. "What do you not get Waleek? The reason we broke up is because you don't think! And you're drama! That bitch over there!" She pointed to where Muff was now standing, after being drug off Braya.

"That bitch is drama! I'm done! D-O-N-E," she spelled out for emphasis.

Waleek looked like, every ounce of pride he possessed, had been stripped from him. He hated to accept it, but he knew he had to. As bad as Asia was, and as much as he wanted her; he wasn't going to chase. He stood there and paused for a minute.

"Whatever yo. Fuck you then," he mumbled dejectedly, before backing up and walking off.

"Fuck you too nigga," Asia huffed, before turning her back and walking up the street to her truck.

"Damn," she mumbled. *Mufucka's act like they can't handle rejection nowadays*, she thought. *I got the nerve*, she thought. Thoughts of her pathetic ass standing on the curb pleading to Josiah surfaced to her mind; however, she quickly pushed them to the rear of her thought. She thought back to Waleek.

It didn't make any sense to her, that she had to go through all that bullshit for him to finally get the hint. She looked down the street and couldn't help but notice Braya limping to her car. Muff had beat the brakes off her. She was a hot mess. Her clothes were ripped and her hair standing on top of her head. Waleek was no longer in sight. He didn't even help her busted ass to the car. *That's what the bitch gets. Worried about some black ass dick got her beat the fuck up,* she thought. *Trifling bitch.*

Asia started her truck up and headed home. She prayed it was the last time she ever saw Braya, Waleek, or Muff's crazy ass again. It was crazy how her life had once again been turned upside down in a matter of weeks. As usual ... it was behind someone else's bullshit. She was tired of going through things for other people and *with* other people. She just wanted to be happy and start truly living. During the course of each of her relation-ships; she could have picked up and walked away. However, she chose to stay out of loyalty for someone else. When Mitch got locked up, she could have walked away. When Waleek was taking her through Hell, she could have walked away. When Josiah came into her world and offered her a new life, she could have walked away. It was time for her to start living for herself ... and finally do some damn walking.

🎋 23 🎋

"**D**amn," Mitch sighed, after receiving the news from Asia. He ran his hand over his head in frustration. It wasn't what he expected when Asia walked through the door. If it wasn't one thing, it was another.

"So why don't you just hire one?" Mitch asked.

"Because it's not in the center's budget," Asia replied. "A Daycare Director in Philly is running around $50,000 a year. Most of the smaller daycare's like mine, are usually owned and operated by someone who can also serve as a director. It's just not in my budget. That's 100k a year ... That's like adding four full-time employees. Two additional employees per center. I just can't afford that," she admitted solemnly. "I don't know what I'm going to do."

For the first time in a while, Mitch felt like less of a man. He had money, but there was no long-term fix for what Asia needed. Besides, with his mounting legal fees, he had to account for every dollar that he spent. He had to make a move and make a move soon. With the daycare's closed, Asia once again had zero income coming in. That meant that he was soon going to be footing every single one of her bills and paying the lawyer fees. He didn't mind taking care of Asia. She didn't have a heavy overhead. His concern was the leases weren't out on either of her locations. Despite being shut down; she would still have to pay her monthly rent on both properties.

He needed a connect. As promised, Pop had hit him earlier and told him that he knew someone that could get a larger amount of work to him. It was a guy from Germantown that he knew. Although Asia had been born and raised on that side of Philadelphia, he himself wasn't familiar with too many niggas from the area. Because of this, he knew he had to be extra careful. He needed a larger inflow of money, and despite his reluctance, he was going to proceed. Pop vouched for him, and that said a lot since Pop was his right-hand man. The same careful measurements that he used were the same ones that Pop considered as well.

Mitch looked over to Asia who was now sitting at the kitchen table with her head resting slightly in her hands. He could tell she was worried and that bothered him. This wouldn't be a worry if Josiah was still in the picture and he knew that.

"Look I'm going to take care of it. Don't worry okay," he said. "You know I got you," he added

Asia lifted her head up and responded. "Thanks, Mitch. Just make sure you stay on point and don't get in any trouble," she said.

Mitch had already briefed her on the connect from out of G-town. Since she was from there, he figured she might have known the nigga in question. She had heard the name, but unfortunately, she didn't know too much about him. His name was Fats. Asia heard he was a heavy hitter in the street; however, she'd only seen him in passing. Waleek had spoken of him several times. He had personally expressed how he didn't care too much for him, without going into details. Despite his feelings, Asia had never heard about him doing any bad business. She was actually surprised that Mitch was going to him for weight. She expected for him to seek out a much larger connect. Someone like Josiah.

But, she guessed there weren't too many Josiah's just laying around.

Calling it a night, Asia decided to head to bed. She had a headache, and she needed some rest after the day's events. Hasan was already in bed, so she kissed Mitch good night, and headed to the shower so she could prepare to lay down. Mitch, however, wasn't ready to go to sleep. He instead called Pop.

"What's up my nigga," Mitch asked. "I'm gonna go ahead and go through with what we talked about earlier. How soon do you think you can line that shit up?" he asked.

Mitch hoped that he could arrange a meeting for tomorrow but to his surprise, Pop revealed that Fats was on standby and could be ready for him in an hour or two. That was all Mitch needed to hear. After he hung up, he grabbed Asia's keys off the kitchen table and headed out to meet Pop first. They would drive to Germantown together to meet Fats. Time was money, and he couldn't afford to be a minute late. He had to make moves. Everything was riding on him now.

❧ 24 ❧

An hour later, Lil' Baby pumped softly through the speakers and Pop sat quietly in the passenger seat while Mitch focused on getting them to their destination.

"Why you so quiet nigga?" Mitch asked. "I thought you and yo' nigga's would be excited that yo came through so quick with the work."

"Hell yeah. They're ready. My stomach just hurtin' a little bit after taking down a half bottle of Hennessy earlier," he admitted.

"Damn. Ol' baby belly ass nigga," Mitch chuckled. "You know yo' ass can't handle liquor for shit."

He glanced over at Pop who had his phone in his hand and was texting.

"That nigga there already?" he asked, glancing from the road to Pop.

"Yeah. Tryin' figure out where we at," he said softly.

Mitch figured that much. Pop had been texting since he hopped in the car. The drive was a relatively short one since they only had to go from Southwest to Germantown. That was only about ten minutes on the Schuylkill.

"Tell him we'll be there in five minutes."

Mitch turned the music up and hit the gas on Asia's truck.

Although it was the city, the expressway was still quiet, allowing him to seize the roadway. Before they knew it, Mitch had taken exit 1 and was now driving around the deserted streets of Germantown.

"Where the fuck this shit at?" Mitch frowned, after seemingly driving around aimlessly for the past couple minutes. Pop was trying to rattle off an address, but it wasn't popping up properly in the GPS.

"I thought you said you been here before."

"Nigga, I have. It's dark. I don't fuck with Germantown like that. I'm a Southwest nigga just like you," he added sharply. "Plus, this shit looks weird as fuck at night. Just pull over and let me call the nigga real quick. We not far."

"Alright but hurry the fuck up," he said.

He had too much money in his trunk to be pulled over on the side of a shitty ass street in a foreign area. It wasn't that he was scared; he was cautious. Mitch pulled over on the side of the street and threw his car in park while Pop called Fats.

"Yeah, where you at? Damn. We just passed that. Alright cool. We on our way. We only a couple minutes away," Pop said before hanging up and throwing his phone into the pocket of his black hoodie.

"Where he at?" Mitch asked.

"Fernhill Park."

"I thought he had a spot out here? Why the fuck this nigga wanna meet in a park?" Mitch asked curiously, his eyebrows instantly going up.

He started his car up and spun his car around for a U-turn back in the direction they had come. He knew where Fernhill park was, so he no longer needed Pop's sorry-ass directions.

"This where y'all met up last time?" Mitch asked out of instinct.

"Yeah. He solid. I told you I vouch for him," Pop added.

The words Pop spoke caused an eerie chill to sweep through Mitch. Pop was lying. He had told Mitch that he spoke to Fats on the phone a few days ago, and then met him at the home of another nigga he claimed he knew since the sandbox. Someone else he claimed to vouch for. Now all of a sudden, he had met him in the park. Something wasn't right. He hated to think that Pop was on some nut shit, but his gut never failed him. In all his life ... his gut had never lied to him one time.

"Na, I ain't wit' it," Mitch said casually.

If it didn't feel right, he wasn't going to do it.

"I'll find a connect somewhere else," he said simply, without hinting that he felt that Pop was actually up to something. However, because they had been friends so long, Pop knew when Mitch was suspicious.

Mitch slowed to the last stop before the entrance to the expressway. Before he could come to a complete stop, Pop had snatched his gun from his side and had it aimed to the side of Mitch's head. Wasn't nothing coming in between him and his come-up.

"Make this right," Pop said coldly.

Mitch grew quiet but did as instructed. Out of all people ... Pop. He couldn't believe Pop was trying to jack him. Mitch instantly knew it was karma. This would have been Josiah's fate as well if things had gone according to plan. He was so wrapped up with taking down a solid nigga that he had never seen the treacherous scheme being prepared right behind his back.

"What's this about?" Mitch asked.

Although he already knew, he still had to ask. His brain was still having a difficult time registering that his friend since childhood was committing such a larcenous act against him.

"You already know what it's about. Just business baby," Pop replied coolly.

Mitch knew better than anyone that there was no loyalty in the streets. A traitor was often one that was closest to the heart. In the words of the O'Jay's, *For the love of money, people will rob their own brother.*

"Pull up in the park ... Over there by the tree."

As Mitch pulled into the dark, tree-lined park, he headed towards where Pop had told him to drive. The spot in question was deeper into the park; dimly lit and near a dumpster. Mitch also noticed that there was another car. As he drove closer he saw two of Pop's young niggas standing by Pop's own Ford Taurus. Both men looked armed and dangerous. Mitch was no fool. Although his initial plan was to cooperate and just gave them the bread in the trunk, he now knew that they had no intentions of letting him live. They were going to kill him. He didn't want to believe it, but he had no choice. He had to think quickly if he wanted to survive. Pop still had his gun trained on him, but Mitch no longer cared. If he was going to die; he was going to die fighting.

"Pull over and get the fuck out the car," Pop demanded as Mitch slowed to a stop.

He waved for his young boys to supervise Mitch's exit. All it took was for Pop to lower his gun. As soon as he did and then proceeded to grab the door handle to get out, Mitch drew his weapon from his own hoodie.

The force from the barrel of Mitch's gun sent Pop to the ground in a crumpled heap. He spun back around to his own window and Pop's men were already in front of him with the door open. Now that they stood in front of them he recognized them as Bug and Loso. Bug already had his gun pointed on Mitch; however, that didn't stop him from still firing on both their asses. Mitch squeezed his trigger and let out four shots to back them up.

"Fuck! I'm hit," he heard Bug yell out.

Seizing the once in a lifetime opportunity, he snatched the truck's gear out of park, and peeled Asia's truck back wildly in reverse. As he barreled backward out of the gravel park, several bullets from Loso's gun shattered the front windshield causing shards of glass to fly into Mitch's face and eyes. Out of instinct, he lowered his head and tried to wipe the debris out of his face. A second later, while Mitch struggled to flee and maintain control of the vehicle, several more bullets ripped through the interior. Pain traveled through Mitch's body. The unfolding chaos caused him to lose control of the truck, slamming into a light pole.

❦

THE SOUND from the impact and the truck's blaring alarm caused those nearby to awaken out of their sleep. Mitch was too weak to run, and even if he wanted to, the damage from the collision prevented him from getting out to do so. Not only was he stuck; he was also injured. He had been shot in his shoulder, and the pain was so unbearable that he had momentarily slipped out of consciousness. Mitch had no doubt that his collar bone was broken. He didn't know if it had come from the crash or the gunshot. As he sat stuck in the truck, he didn't know what to do. He had no way out, and once again he had failed Asia. He had to call her and let her know what was going on. Despite everything that had just taken place, Mitch spotted his cell phone right away. He reached over painfully and grabbed it.

He was about to instruct his iPhone to call Asia, but then he stopped. He didn't want to wake her with bad news. He was tired of putting her through that. She had enough going on. She'd just lost her businesses, and now she was going to lose him. He knew he was going to jail. The way her truck was mangled into the pole; there was no way he was getting out without the help of firefighters. He decided to make a call to someone else instead. His whole purpose on the dangerous streets of Philadelphia was to provide for his family. As the police sirens grew alarmingly close; he made the phone call that he knew would ensure that.

❧ 25 ❧

Josiah stood alone once again, staring out the window of his condo in downtown Wilmington. The twins were sleep, and his mother and sister were both up watching television in the living room nearby. He'd already had his drink, so this time he had nothing to sip on while he stared at the river. His mind was swirling with thoughts, while his heart roared with emotion. He didn't know what had become of his life. He had so much, but it wasn't enough. *Or was it?* He didn't know if he was being ungrateful. He'd hustled most of his adult life, had a shit-load of money ... but no one to share it with. He wondered what life had in store for him. Was he being punished? Was this the cost that he would be forced to pay for years of illegally obtaining wealth. If it was, it wasn't worth it.

His thoughts drifted to Trish. A part of him wanted to say, "fuck it" and settle down with her. Have some kids. However, another part of him couldn't see himself subjecting himself to a life of misery. Perhaps he could learn to be happy with her. *Fuck that*, he thought. Albeit a good woman, Josiah refused to settle. He believed in love. If he couldn't have it with Asia, then he would just wait for it. Just as his mind jumped to the next thought, he felt his phone begin to vibrate in his pocket. He pulled it out and looked at the time. Mitch never called him that late. He wondered what the fuck was up. He quickly answered.

"Hello?"

"I need your help," Mitch replied weakly. "Look," Mitch paused. "I know about you and Asia. I know that she loves you, and I need you to do me a favor."

Josiah went to respond, but Mitch cut him off.

"I got robbed and shot trying to get a new connect. I got one but banged out trying to get away. I'm hurt, and I can't get the fuck out. Cops is pulling up so I'm getting booked for this. Go get my family man," Mitch begged. "Make them yours. Take care of them. You have my blessing. Let her know that since I know that's important to her."

"Is there anything I can do for you?" Josiah asked. The situation sounded bad.

"If you love her, just take care of them," he reiterated.

"You got my word," Josiah said.

The two hung up, and for a few minutes, Josiah simply stood there and gripped his phone tightly. Asia had never told him that she had informed Mitch of their relationship. He had no clue what God was doing, but he damn sure planned to make the most of it.

"I gotta run somewhere," he told his sister and mother once he finally emerged away from the window and back into the living room.

"At this time of night? You know our flight leaves at six," Lolita complained. She looked up into Josiah's face, and her look of annoyance changed to concern. She instantly knew something was wrong. "Is everything okay?" she asked.

"Yeah. I just gotta handle something important," he said, before grabbing his jacket and heading to Philadelphia.

❧ 26 ❧

"Are you fuckin' crazy!" Asia threw her hand to her mouth to muffle her scream as she kicked and scrambled up out of bed and against her headboard.

She had woken to find Josiah gently shaking her awake. He had terrified her. Her chest hammered as she struggled to control her racing heart.

"What are you doing here! You scared me half to death," she said through clenched teeth. Her eyes darted to her bedroom door. "Where's Mitch?" she demanded to know.

"That's why I'm here," he said solemnly.

"What happened?" A new kind of fear now washed over her. "Where is he?"

Josiah looked down at Asia and was unsure how to tell her what Mitch told him. He would do the best he could.

"Mitch was robbed last night while he was going to meet a new connect?"

"Pop?" Asia asked in disbelief.

She couldn't believe what she was hearing. She didn't even need to know all the details. Josiah had just said Mitch was going to meet a connect. The only person he was with, was Pop. If anyone tried to rob him, it had to have been him. She couldn't believe Pop would do something like that.

"Is he ... Is he?" she stammered.

"He's not dead."

Relief instantly washed over Asia.

"He's hurt though," he continued. "He was shot and wrecked the whip while he tried to get away. When he called me, I could hear police sirens in the back. They'll probably take him to the hospital to treat him and then they're going to book him. You know how the rest goes."

"Do you know what he's going to be charged with?" she asked, her heart falling to her feet.

"I don't know. He did say he killed one of them."

"Wait ... One of them?"

It was all too much for Asia to take in. *There was more than one robber?* she thought. Pop had help. *What the hell is going on?* She thought. She instantly scrambled from her bed and ran to turn on the light. She wanted to grab her phone so she could at least call Mitch. She needed answers.

"I need to talk to Mitch," she said, before suddenly beginning to sob.

She couldn't help but break down. It was all too much. Months and months of setbacks, heartache, and anguish. She couldn't do it anymore. Josiah rose up from where he was seated and walked over to Asia to comfort her. He wrapped his arms around her, and she instantly knew everything was going to be okay. She fell into his chest and wept loudly.

"I'm so tired Josiah," she cried.

"I know," he said.

For a few minutes, all he did was stand there and held her while she cried. When her cries started to subside, he spoke.

"He asked me to take care of y'all. He said to tell you that we have his blessing," he quietly.

Asia pulled her head away from Josiah's chest and looked up into his face to see if he was for real. He was.

"I can't do this shit anymore here. I just want to start over," she admitted. She pulled away and looked at him. Her face tear-streaked and sincere.

"Wherever you want to go. I'll have you there tomorrow if you want. First-class," he said.

"I want to leave tonight."

She'd had enough of Philadelphia. To keep from going crazy, she needed to get away as soon as possible.

"Get dressed," he said.

She didn't have to be told twice. An hour later, with her son sleeping safely in Josiah's arms, the three of them boarded a first-class flight to the Sunshine State.

❧ 27 ❧

Asia let out a slight groan as she stirred awake and struggled to peel open her eyes and absorb the sunlight that was seeping into them. She looked at the clock that was right beside her on the nightstand. It was twelve in the afternoon. Asia pushed herself up into the bed in a panic. After about thirty seconds, she remembered where she was at and why she was where she was. She had nowhere to be. No daycare to run. Now she remembered exactly why she was so tired. She looked down to her side. Her son was sleeping peacefully on his back, with the king-sized comforter lying snugly against him.

Asia stared around the room and took in her surroundings. When they came in last night, it was dark. She remembered Josiah telling her to get comfortable. *This is your new home, for now*, he would say to her. She was overwhelmed by everything that had transpired, but she knew she was safe. She remembered the phone call from Mitch. It had come in around 5 a.m. from his hospital bed. She had his blessing to move forward with Josiah. He had given it before, but this time was different. All Mitch wanted was for his family to be taken care of. It was a bittersweet moment. She loved him so much and didn't want to see him back in prison, but she was finally free. She planned to make the most of it; for her and her son.

Asia got out of the bed, being careful not to wake Hasan. He was in his terrible two stage, so every minute he was sleep, was like a physical and mental vacation for her. As she walked around the room, she couldn't believe how massively comfortable it was. It had two walk-in closets, as well as a private master bath. She took a final glance at Hasan and tiptoed into the hallway. Asia couldn't help but notice the place was very quiet, so she decided to give herself a grand tour. She remembered Josiah saying that because they had taken an early flight out, his family would arrive later on their original flight. For a little while, they would have the house to themselves.

As she wandered around, she quickly realized that Josiah had spared no expense. His home in Wilmington was nice, but this place was stunning. The exotic two-story, Spanish-style property was lined with palm trees and had to be around 7,000 square feet. It was in a gated community and was bright and airy, with large, inviting windows sprinkled throughout. She walked through the kitchen and walked outside to the stone patio where she saw expensive outdoor furniture tastefully decorating the area. She looked around at the beautiful view. From a distance, she could see a sparkling lake in the center of the community along with a golf course. On Josiah's own property, there was an inground swimming pool and a basketball court with a small playground attached. *A bitch could get used to this*, she thought. Although she didn't love Josiah for his money; she certainly could appreciate it.

Just as Asia was done looking around, she noticed a car pull up. Since she was still outside admiring the grounds, she was the very first thing that the three women noticed when they exited out of their SUV. She quickly scurried back inside through the patio door. Josiah was sitting in the living room watching television as she crept up behind him. Before Asia could announce her presence, the front door was opening, and his mother Lolita walked in.

"Josiah, wake up!" Lolita called out to him, before briskly walking over to him and shaking him out of his sleep.

"Hey Ma," he replied groggily, still slightly confused.

"What is she doing here? Why didn't you tell me she was coming?" It wasn't that she didn't want her there; she would have just been prepared.

Before Josiah could respond, Asia emerged from the kitchen into the living room. At the same time, the twins came barreling through the front door and then, in walked his sister Maria with Trish beside her. Suddenly, the events from earlier registered and he remembered that he had his queen back with him. Josiah wiped his eyes and prepared to advise everyone of what was going on. He was done explaining himself. He instead was going to lay it all on the line. Whoever didn't like it, was just going to have to deal with it.

"Hey sis. Hey Trish."

The two women stopped near the doorway while Asia walked further into the living room. Her eyes scanned the room until they landed on Trish, who was staring her up and down in contempt.

"Asia this is Trish, and Trish this is Asia. Trish is my sister's best friend. She's like family although we dated," he clarified. "And everyone, this is my future wife, Asia. She and her son are going to be staying with us for a while until I find *us* a place."

Trish shot him a dirty look that Asia couldn't help but catch. Everyone saw it, and she was sure that everyone felt it.

"I ask that you make her feel welcome," Josiah continued.

He looked to Asia, who was standing at his side.

"Our home is your home," he said with finality.

Asia smiled nervously. The look on everyone's face didn't necessarily corroborate that notion. Josiah looked at everyone, and although he hated what the situation was doing to Trish, he had to say it. It was time for the two of them to move on. If

Trish wanted to hate him, she could. However, it was time for them to move on. They had tried it, and it didn't work. Being bitter wasn't going to solve anything.

"I'm gonna go," Trish said. "I'll call you later Maria," she said, before walking out. Maria went running behind her, but Lolita stopped her.

"Let her go. I'm tired of that," she admitted. "She needs to grow up."

Lolita walked slowly to the couch and took a seat and kicked off her shoes. She was exhausted. They'd just gotten in from a three-hour flight and all she wanted to do was relax. Josiah wasn't answering his phone, so Maria insisted that they call Trish to bring them home. After several unnecessary stops they were finally home. She didn't have the energy to run down Trish and wipe her tears every time something went wrong with Josiah. When Lolita was comfortable on the love seat, she turned and faced Josiah with a weary sigh. Asia had walked off to check on Hasan and Maria had left to get the twins situated.

"I'm not going to ask you what happened between her and your friend. All I'm going to ask you is that you're sure about all of this, considering the situation? I know I asked you before, but I'm going to ask you again. Are you sure you love her?"

Josiah didn't hesitate to respond.

"I want to spend my life with her. Have a family with her. So, yes. Yes I do love her," he said.

"Well then ... We will learn to love her too." She smiled at her son warmly.

Josiah returned the smile. Although it wouldn't have affected his desire to be with Asia, having his family's support meant a lot to him. He knew his mother would set the example and Maria would eventually come around.

"Do you think this is going to drive a wedge between Trish and Maria?" he asked.

"Yeah, but don't you worry about that. That wedge was drawn a long time ago," she huffed. "Ever since you two didn't work out the first time, Trish has been unloading her bitterness onto Maria. I told her that at some point, she was going to have to mourn the death of their friendship. I know she loves Trish, but her loyalty is to her family. Besides, I don't trust Trish," Lolita said.

Something told her that Trish wasn't going to take this new relationship between Josiah and Asia lying down.

❧ 28 ❧

The sound of her Christian Louboutin heels clicked against the pavement as Trish headed up the steps and into the big brick Federal courthouse building with Tim walking briskly by her side. Once they walked in and began navigating the halls, Tim shot her a look of reassurance. Their arrival solidified a new beginning. Trish was officially saying goodbye to her old life and emerging into a new one. She would also be saying goodbye to old friends. They would soon be new enemies. The second look Tim sent to her when she glanced in his direction assured her she was doing the right thing. After walking down a long hall, Tim stopped in front of the office they were looking for. It was the office of the federal prosecutor who had been assigned to their case.

"Are you ready to do this?" he asked her.

His face was serious with a hint of warmth. He wanted to make sure she knew that he had her back no matter what.

"Yeah."

She wanted to go ahead and get the shit done and over with so she could move forward with her life. Trish took a deep breath and followed Tim into the office. The man sitting inside greeted them and motioned for them to sit.

"Thank you for coming," he said, hopping up to greet them. "And thank you for accepting the offer that I laid out for you. Do you have any questions before we get started?" he asked.

"Before my client says a word, I need to know that she will be given full immunity."

⚜

MITCH ADJUSTED his body for what seemed like the hundredth time. He was back at the city jail that he had recently called home only a few years back. Only this time, instead of being housed in general population, he was in the infirmary healing from a gunshot wound. He was initially taken to Einstein Hospital, where he was treated for the gunshot wound to his shoulder, as well as a broken collar bone. Despite his battered condition, the cops still questioned him and charged him with a double homicide. When the police had arrived, Pop was dead on the scene and Bug would later succumb to his injuries as he was being transported by paramedics. Mitch knew he was in deep shit. His bail had been revoked, he was fighting an appeal, and now he was being charged with a double homicide. That alone was a couple hundred thousand in legal fees. It was far too much to think about, so he chose not to think at all. He just wanted to sleep. Fortunately for him, the meds they had him on, helped him do just that.

Mitch finally dozed off and had been sleeping for several hours when he was awakened by a knock on the door. In walked two detectives. Mitch knew law enforcement when he saw them, only these guys looked different. As they entered and began shuffling around the room, they hit the light switch. Mitch smacked his teeth and squinted in pain from the blinding light.

"What?" he asked. "I already answered all the questions I'm going to answer. Anything else you motherfuckas wanna know, needs to be directed at my attorney."

He still had no idea how he was even going to get one. The

cops had likely confiscated all the money in Asia's mangled truck, and there was no way he was going to ask her to come out her pockets to help him on this one.

"We aren't here for that," the taller officer replied. "We're Feds. And we have some questions to ask you."

Normally, Mitch would have stopped them; however, out of curiosity, he wanted to hear them out.

"We're working to build a case against Josiah Hernandez. We were informed by an informant that you were familiar with him. He was your supplier."

Mitch gave him a vacant stare. He wasn't sure if the pig in front of him wanted him to confirm that or not. If so ... they had him fucked up. He was no rat, and the only reason he was entertaining their ridiculous chatter was out of curiosity."

"I'm sure you've done your homework. I know him," he admitted. "We were locked up together. Actually, we were locked up *here* together. Cell buddies. That was the extent of our relationship."

"Look. I understand the culture," the shorter detective interjected. "The whole, stop snitching campaign. But this is real life. Your life. You're looking at a lot of time. You're appealing a murder case. You have a new one looming over your head, and you're probably gonna be flat broke real soon because you can't make any money while sitting in a jail cell. You can tell us what you really know about Mr. Hernandez, or you can sit in here and rot," he said with finality.

Mitch paused for a minute. With a sneer, he finally responded.

"I'll rot first. Now get the fuck out my room," he demanded.

Realizing he wasn't going to be any assistance to them, the two detectives left. However, they were just getting started. With the information they had obtained from their key informant; they had a list of names to go off. They were now headed down and through the state of Delaware.

WHILE ASIA LAY face down with her ass hiked up in the air on the large bed, Josiah dove in and out of her moisture. As he continued to stroke in and out of her, he reached down and gripped her breast playfully. As he began planting kisses up and down her back, he realized how much he'd missed her in so many ways. He could tell from the way her canal was gripping his shaft, that she hadn't been tampered with. God was good.

Damn, it's been too long, he thought. Asia moaned in pleasure from his force and touch. She hadn't been handled in so long and Josiah was making it well worth the wait. Josiah continued to dip in and out of her until they both shuddered in unison and collapsed onto the damp sheets.

"You miss me?" she asked with a giggle as he lay on top of her and cuffed her up in his big, strong arms.

"You already," he said.

He closed his eyes to rest them briefly, but Asia began shaking her body to wake him up.

"Un-un. You not 'bout to fall asleep on me. I gotta take a quick shower and then go check on Hasan," she said. Josiah was good for climbing his gigantic ass on top of her and falling asleep, leaving her stuck up under him. *Not today*, she thought.

"Hasan is fine. He's playing with the twins."

"Yeah, I'm sure he's fine, but I'm his mother, and I'm going to check on him."

Josiah snatched his arm from under her and rolled off of her and onto his back. Asia scurried to the bathroom, while Josiah attempted to get a quick nap. He didn't care if he was sweaty or not. As long as he had been away from Asia, he didn't mind marinating in her juices. Before he could settle his eyes, his phone began vibrating from the nightstand.

Josiah reached over and grabbed it. He recognized the number as the city jail in Philadelphia. He quickly answered it.

Once the recording finished, Mitch was on the line, speaking very quickly.

"Hey Josiah. Wassup, boi. I'm gon' make this real quick. I need you to listen to me. The FEDS came and questioned me today about you. I can't say anything else and neither should you. Get up with your lawyer. How's Asia and my son?" he asked.

"They're good as promised. I'll make sure they stay good. Do you need anything?" Josiah asked.

"Na, I'm good. I just wanted to hit you and hip you to that visit. Get on that asap," he said.

The two ended their call and Josiah sat up in the bed. *Why the fuck would the FEDS have gone to see Mitch?* he thought. He wasn't worried about them talking to Mitch since he knew that he would never open his mouth. However, he needed to figure out who did. There was no reason that the FEDS should be questioning anyone about him. He wondered if it had something to do with Ethan. He needed to call his lawyer. Someone other than Tim.

Later that evening, Asia and Josiah sat on the patio and enjoyed the warm weather. Although his mind was racing, he did his best not to project any negative energy or any indication that he was stressed. He wanted to do things differently than the way Mitch had. His struggles and legal issues would be his alone. He didn't come into her life to make it stressful. That wasn't his goal. He wanted to instead make her life meaningful.

"So, did you take care of everything with the daycares back in Philly?" he asked. It had only been a few days, but he wanted to make sure she left no loose ends.

"Yeah, I informed my staff. Luckily, the daycare business is booming in Philly, so they won't be out of work long. I still feel so bad. I wasn't even open long. I feel like a failure. Letting all those parents down. My staff," she said solemnly, as she nuzzled against Josiah's taut chest.

"Don't feel like that. You're still young. You didn't fail, you just caught a setback is all. We're going to go over to the bank, and I'm going to wire some money from my account to yours. I want to make sure you have your own," he said.

Asia went to interject, but Josiah cut her off.

"Hear me out," he said. "I know you have a little money, but it's not enough. If anything ever happens to me, I want to make sure you can take care of yourself. If someone tries to throw you out, I want you to be able to walk out gracefully with your middle finger up because you'll have enough cash to buy whatever you want ... *flat the fuck out*. And that includes a crib. You can sell your condo or keep it. That money is yours. I also want you to go get a lawyer. A real lawyer that you can have on standby. Some shit happens, and all you have to do is make one phone call. That lawyer is gon' pull up. Once I get you some more money over, we're going to find out how much it's going to be to get you out of your building contracts in Philly. If they won't let you out, have them find a way to settle it. I'll make sure that it's taken care of."

"Josiah, you don't have to do all this," she said.

"I know, but everybody that I love is taken care of. My mother, my sister, my nieces; everybody. Everything they have belongs to them. My sister has a shoe fetish, so she owns boutiques in Miami. You love children, so as soon as you take care of things in Philly, we'll get you going down here. You won't be leasing a building though. You'll buy one."

"Thank you, Josiah," she said quietly. She wanted to ask him something, but she didn't know how he would take it. "I have a request," she finally said.

"I think I know what it is, but I'll let you ask."

"Mitch's legal fees ..." She paused. "I can't afford them. It's probably going to be a couple hundred thousand."

"I'll take care of them. I had planned to anyway."

"Thank you," she said.

Josiah leaned over and gave her a kiss.

"Anything for you." In death or in jail, he was going to make sure that she was taken care of. He prayed that it didn't come to the jail part. He was going to meet with his lawyer in the morning to find out what was going on. He prayed it wasn't too bad.

29

Lolita stroked Josiah's back gently as he sat in the plush leather seats across from his high-profile lawyer and struggled to take everything in. Although everything was coming as a shock to Josiah, Lolita had been preparing for this moment. She knew it was going to come. Trish was trying to take down her son. After his phone call with Mitch, Josiah only informed Lolita of what was going on. It wasn't that he wanted her to share his burden; he just knew that she would have been upset if he had left her in the dark about what was taking place. Knowing what he was up against, she insisted on accompanying him to meet with the lawyer. Pretending to have a mother and son day, they were able to get out of the house without arising anyone's suspicions.

"What else do they have," he asked solemnly. He now was hunched over running his hands across his face to see if he would wake up. It felt like a bad dream.

"Right now, all they have is her statement. They probably offered her immunity. It's also likely that with her deal, Ethan would also walk. Now, there are several ways that this could go," his lawyer began. "Her testimony isn't enough for a conviction. The FEDS aren't going to try anything in court that they aren't certain they're going to win. With just her statement, they don't have enough. Ethan doesn't know anything. If it remains that way, they will likely hold off. This is where they would keep digging. Keep watching to try to build a case against you. You aren't being charged with anything right now. But ... you are under surveillance. Another way this could play out is everyone that Trish implicated could roll on you. She gave them a list. Your buddy that called; his name was one of the ones on it. She said you helped him run a prison drug ring. She also said that you supplied people all throughout Delaware."

Josiah swallowed the hard lump that had formed in his throat. The odds were starting to stack against him. He looked to his side at his mother. Her face showed disappointment.

"If they can get more witnesses to corroborate her claim, they can start to build their case. FED cases are a little harder to build. Since they didn't catch you with anything, it makes it even harder. They also base a lot of their investigation and prosecution on wiretaps. At this point, they don't have any of those either. This is a fairly new investigation. We usually don't find out someone is working with the Feds until it's far too late. To be honest, when they contacted Mitch, they fumbled their entire case. If they had done their homework properly, they would know that he doesn't seem like the type of guy to start talking."

"Well ... Let's say, worst comes to worse, and a couple people *or all the people* on that list confirm that she is telling the truth and say that I did supply them. What would happen?"

"You could be facing federal distribution charges. But, to be honest, I don't think that's going to happen. None of the people named on the list have pending court cases. None of them were caught with drug's recently. Most people give up names when they're busted or caught red-handed with drugs. That isn't the case here. No one is going to incriminate themselves willingly Even if they catch them later, you've already admitted to me that you're out of the drug game. They're no longer getting drugs from you. So, if they're caught later, they can't point the finger at you and say that's where they got it. Even if we're faced with the worst-case scenario, they have to get in that courthouse and prove beyond a reasonable doubt that you distributed drugs to them. A good friend of mine is one of the top Federal Criminal Defense Lawyers on the East Coast. He'd slaughter Trish's character ... because clearly she's doing this out of spite. Sure she wants to help Ethan, but she also wants to take down a man that she loves that doesn't love her back."

"So, what's the next step?" Lolita asked, finally speaking up.

"All we can do is wait. I do want to also add that this information is classified. I have a connection with the Federal prosecution. Don't speak on this to anyone. Don't talk over the phones and don't sell any drugs. Don't talk about drugs and don't mention drugs."

"Okay," Josiah agreed. Luckily, all those things would be easy for him. Josiah and his mother got up to leave but was stopped abruptly by their new attorney Sam.

"Oh, and I forgot to add. Don't be surprised if they find another way to get to you if this drug shit doesn't work. From what we discussed earlier; you have a lot of assets. They may make you break down your income and how you acquired everything. So ... don't be surprised if they try to instead hit you with money laundering."

Josiah and Lolita left quietly. They weren't too worried about the money laundering. He had a crooked lawyer that cleaned his money to make everything look legit. Lolita had demanded it years ago just in case something like this happened. When they got back in the car and began heading back to their home in Ft. Lauderdale, Josiah glanced at his mother in the passenger seat. She was worried.

"I want to talk to Trish," she said.

"Mommy, you know that isn't a good idea," Josiah said. "It's only going to make things worse."

"I just don't understand how she could do something like

this. I never trusted her, but I didn't speak on it as hard as I could, because Maria loved her." She shook her head tearfully. "Now look."

"Don't stress about it. You know I grind to take care of y'all. Y'all taken care of. They'll never convict on a money laundering case. Y'all assets legit. The drugs are another story. Worst case scenario, I'll take a plea. I'm a man."

"I know baby, but I'm still angry and this shit breaks my heart." She paused for a minute. "Are you going to tell Asia what's going on?"

"I'm going to have to at some point. Depends on how far the Feds go. How much they find out. I don't want to worry her. I brought her down here for a fresh start and that's what I intend to give her. All I ask is ... If I get jammed up and sentenced behind this shit; that you all continue to show her love and support."

"Of course honey. And you know your sister will eventually come around."

Maria had been having a hard time accepting Asia, especially since Trish had seemingly shut her out since her arrival. Trish had changed her number and was no longer responding to messages from her so-called "best-friend."

"Are you going to tell her?" he asked.

"I'm going to have to. She needs to know."

❧

SEVERAL MONTHS HAD PASSED, and Asia was settling in Ft. Lauderdale nicely and was loving every bit of it. The sunny skies, beautiful weather, and carefree living; she couldn't get enough of it. Life was completely different. She'd gotten out of her building contracts with ease, was enrolled in college, and was officially a millionaire. Josiah had made her one in the blink of an eye when he wired one million dollars to her bank account. She had no idea he had that type of money. That quickly, her life changed.

She now had a home in the same neighborhood as Josiah's mother and a brand new, candy apple red Mercedes to go with it. The materials weren't even what made Asia feel whole. It was the way that Josiah encouraged her to be her best self. After going through issues with her daycares in Philly, Josiah insisted that she get her degree before she opened another one, so she enrolled in nearby Nova Southeastern University to study Education. She was only a few weeks in, but she knew going back to school was one of the best decisions she'd ever made.

Josiah had even encouraged her to make amends with her mother. Although Sheila had her ways, she was still the woman that had raised her. She was still family. Asia loved how family-oriented he and his family were. Her and Lolita were now thick as thieves, and Maria had even come around. Her and Asia now got along beautifully. Maria even helped her brother surprise Asia with a trip to Mexico for her 23rd birthday. Since they all adored Hasan and he got along beautifully with the twins; they volunteered to keep him the entire week Asia and Josiah soaked up the sun and enjoyed her birthday. They had just returned and were now unpacking.

"Oh yeah, I forgot to tell you that Mitch called," Josiah said as they settled into the master bedroom of their new home.

Instead of calling Asia constantly, Mitch was being respectful and reaching out to Josiah instead. He still communicated with her and spoke to his son; however, he didn't want to be a factor in their relationship. He had matured a lot and was holding himself responsible for all his choices and actions. He was also being more mindful about how those actions affected the ones he loved and cared for. For the first time in a long time, he felt bad about what he had done; or more, *what he had to do.* Although Pop tried to set him up, he still mourned. They had been "friends" for many years. Mitch still had to live with the fact that he had torn apart a family. Pop's mother, his sister, his family; they were all heartbroken and confused over the loss.

Although Mitch knew the true story; he had to accept the fact that they would hate him forever for taking his life.

"What he talkin' bout?" Asia asked.

She dug through her suitcase and began separating clean items from unclean items.

"They offered him a plea. Three years for the handgun."

"Wow," was all she could say as she stopped digging. "Did he say what he was going to do?"

"He's going to take it. That's not bad. He made out pretty damn good," Josiah admitted. "That was the minimum they had to give him since he was a felon with a handgun. The homicide charges would be dismissed."

"You're right. That is good," she agreed.

With Josiah's financial assistance, Mitch had also won his appeal. His previous sentence had been vacated and he only had to deal with the current charges where he had been robbed and shot. Josiah made sure to hire Mitch the best attorney in the tri-county area, and after $150,000 in legal fees, he got to walk away with just three years. Although some would say that was still a lot of time, Mitch was cool with it. He had taken two lives and would be released in two years. It was a small victory for everyone. He would now have a fresh start. This time he planned to make the most of it.

❧ 30 ❧

"**D**id they say how the case against Josiah is coming along?" Trish asked Tim.

Tim sighed in aggravation at her thought pattern. He had just finished eating her out, and she wanted to talk about Josiah. They'd been sleeping together on and for years, and Trish was still the same way. He knew she was only using him for a quick fuck, but he didn't care. He loved Trish. Had since college. He never understood what she saw in Josiah. Tim too was handsome. He stood at 5'11, creamy skin, with dark hair; he had all the female associates at his law firm going crazy. However, he didn't want anyone else but Trish. She was beautiful and intelligent, but ... she was bitter and still in love with a drug dealer.

"Yeah, actually," he said. He continued to button up his dress shirt so he could get going. He would have preferred to stay the night, but Trish never allowed it.

"*Well* ..." she said, encouraging him to spill the beans. She had to know.

"They're at a standstill."

"What? A standstill?" she asked in disbelief. "What does that mean. I gave them over a half dozen names on that list." She let

162

out an exasperated sigh and ran her hand through her disheveled hair.

Tim stopped fumbling with his shirt and looked at Trish worriedly. She was getting worse by the day. She'd been drinking and isolating herself, and if he didn't know any better, he'd say she was on some heavy drugs. He knew very soon he was going to have to get her help. He'd tried reaching out to her mother but since her health had begun failing her, she was now in a nursing home. Trish was the only child so there was no one else to call. Tim kind of thought that was part of the reason for Trish's downfall. She wanted so desperately to have a family.

"No one's talking. Right now, they still have nothing but your testimony. Josiah completely halted his operation, so they have nothing."

"Yeah, I bet," she grumbled bitterly. She knew it was no one other but his bitch of a mother Lolita. She had the final say when it came to everything. Trish knew that Lolita never cared much for her. She honestly believed she was the reason they didn't make it.

"Why do you want to see him fall so bad anyway?" Tim asked. He went back to putting on his things. He was now sitting on the edge of the bed putting on his dress shoes.

"Because he deserves it. He's going to let Ethan take the fall for his drugs. I'm tired of seeing him ruin people's lives. I can't let that happen," she said shaking her head.

Tim stopped and stared at her. "You think he ruined yours?"

"Yeah," she said softly, her eyes welling with tears.

"And why is that?" he asked.

"He just did okay!" she yelled.

"You know what I think?" Tim said. He continued without waiting for a response. "I think you're ruining your own life by sitting in a hotel room wallowing in self-pity."

It was true. Trish had moved from Delaware to Florida and hadn't even found a place of her own. She had claimed to want a fresh start, yet she wasn't taking any steps to achieve it.

"Josiah and his family loved you. From what I saw anyway. Yeah, he fucked you over, used you, and you guys didn't work out. That happens to a lot of women. Trust me, I know them firsthand. The only difference is, he left wealthy. You were still welcome in his home. Look at you. You're a wreck. You barely come out. You won't talk to your only friend. Do you know Maria has been calling me to check on you? But, you probably don't even care. You have a Master's degree in business for God's sake," he argued. "But you'd rather risk your freedom by going and confessing to helping him sell drugs ... For what Patricia? To hurt him, like he hurt you?" he asked.

None of it made sense to him. Everything she wanted with Josiah; she could have with him too. However, he didn't even bother to mention it because he knew that it would go in one ear and out the other.

"Fuck you!" she screamed, hurling a pillow at him.

"Trish ... You need to get some help. Get out of this room and get back out there in the world and live your life," he said sternly.

He loved Trish, but he could no longer watch her like that.

"How about you just leave," she said.

Without protest, Tim left. Had he known how Trish was really doing, he would have stayed. That night she would stay up to the wee hours of the morning and stalk Josiah's Instagram and Facebook page. He wasn't usually big on social media; however, with Asia's insistence, he had learned to use it more frequently. After digging through his latest photos, Trish couldn't accept the fact that he had truly moved on. She had wanted to be with Josiah since she first laid eyes on him in high school. It was all too much for her, so she took a half a bottle of sleeping pills prescribed to her by her doctor. She would never wake up.

EPILOGUE

Josiah and his family were devastated when they learned Trish had died from an overdose. Maria was especially distraught. She felt like she could have done more. However, Lolita assured her that there was nothing more anyone could have done for Trish.

With Trish dead, the prosecution no longer had their witness. While it worked out in Josiah's favor, it didn't necessarily work out for Ethan. He would eventually be handed down a five-year prison sentence for drug trafficking. Although Josiah felt bad, he couldn't bring himself to trade his freedom for Ethan's. He instead had his lawyer donate a half-million dollars to his family. Although it would never compensate for him losing five-years of his life, it would bring him some comfort knowing that it wasn't completely in vain. Josiah was now focused on being an honest man. Asia would help make him one. Once the Feds dropped their pending investigation against him, he surprised her with an engagement ring. Of course, she said yes.

Asia couldn't believe how far God had brought her. From the gritty streets of Philadelphia to the lush city of Ft. Lauderdale; she was thankful. She and Josiah were going to start working on expanding their family after she finished college, and she planned to have daycare centers all through Florida when she was done. One thing she had learned through her 23-year journey was that choices dictated life. As soon as she had the courage to start truly living and making choices that put her first, that is when her life began to change. She vowed to continue putting herself first while continuing to be unapologetic during her pursuit of happiness.

THE END

TEXT TO JOIN

To stay up to date on new releases, plus get exclusive information on contests, sneak peeks, and more...

Text ColeHartSig to (855)231-5230